The Chalk Cross

··⊰[BERTHE AMOSS]⊱··

The Chalk Cross

A Clarion Book · The Seabury Press · New York

The Seabury Press, 815 Second Avenue, New York, N.Y.   10017

Copyright © 1976 by Berthe Amoss
Designed by Aileen Friedman
Printed in the United States of America

Library of Congress Cataloging in Publication Data
Amoss, Berthe.
    The chalk cross.
    "A Clarion book."
    SUMMARY: A young girl living in nineteenth century New Orleans struggles between her growing familiarity with voodoo and the precepts of the church.
    1. Voodooism—Fiction. 2. New Orleans—Fiction
I. Title.
PZ7.A5177Ch   [Fic]   75-4778
ISBN 0-8164-3150-7

In 1832, Père Antoine had been dead three years, and it would be four more years before work on the St. Louis Hotel began. These are facts I've altered knowingly, and, although I hope not, I may have changed a few other minor ones unknowingly, because, most of all, I wanted to give a true impression of a unique place and its diverse people through the eyes of a young girl. An impression of those years still hovers over the city like a benign miasma, bewitching those who live here and some who visit. With affection, I dedicate *The Chalk Cross* to New Orleans.

Contents

Prologue

The caretaker of the St. Louis Cemetery in New Orleans was pulling the summer's growth of weeds out of the cracks in the tomb-house of Marie Laveau, the long-dead Voodoo queen. He crossed himself to ward off her spirit; he, for one, believed that the black magic of the Voodoos was as dead as its queen, but it didn't hurt to play safe.

He shaded his eyes to watch a plane and frowned at the sky—another scorcher of a day. Already, at nine in the morning, the sun-baked stones were putting out a white glare that had him squinting. By afternoon, the sky would be dark with wind-driven thunderheads, ready to pound the city with their heavy load of summer rain, but now, perspiration beaded under his shade hat and rolled down into his eyes.

It was after he'd passed his handkerchief across his forehead that he saw the girl. She was crouched against the door of the tomb. He had not yet opened the gates to visitors; besides, the girl did not look like the tourists who tramped through the cemetery, guidebook in hand, peering at inscriptions and commenting on the quaint ness of the above-ground, houselike tombs. This girl was about fourteen or fifteen years old, he reckoned, with light-brown skin and hair shining black against the whitewashed stone. Mixed blood, he said to himself, probably octoroon.

He asked her name. Sidonie Laveau, daughter of Marie Laveau, she answered weakly. Impossible, of course—she would be one hundred and fifty! She was not trying to make fun of an old man so early in the morning, was she? No, she answered, she knew well enough who she was. When she said her birthday was September 25, 1817, but that it hurt her head to remember, the caretaker hurried to his office at the gate and called for a Charity Hospital ambulance.

But when he returned, the girl was gone. On the stone where she had lain, he saw the Voodoo cross, crudely drawn in red chalk. He kicked dirt into the chalk and quickly crossed himself again, this time with fervor. He had seen such signs on this tomb before.

The Chalk Cross

L'Académie

I walked through the gates and past the porter's lodge of l'Académie aux Bois, Collège des Beaux Arts de la Nouvelle Orléans. Bois it is called for short, and I, Stephanie Martin, was one of its forty new art students, selected from over one thousand applicants for the 1976 term.

Oak trees dappled shadows on Bois's ancient walls as I stood still, staring, trying to believe my good fortune. I had imagined this moment so many times that, now that it was here, I had the feeling I was not myself, that the real me was watching someone else, another girl luckier than I could ever be. The feeling was so strong, I pinched my arm and blinked. The shadows were gone, erased by clouds, but I was still staring at Bois, proud and aloof, a dowager queen, protected by a walled garden and her own inherent dignity.

In the distance, the rumble of thunder hurried me down the brick walk toward the convent entrance. On one side, as old as the building itself and wet-green from a recent sprinkling, was Bois's herb garden. It had been planted by the nuns two hundred and fifty years ago when they crossed the ocean from France to care for and educate young girls of the colony, white, black, Indian alike. This same order of nuns still administered Bois, and one of them was walking between the rows, snipping a bouquet, and coming toward me.

"Rosemary," she said, holding out a little branch of spiky leaves. "For remembrance, you know." A pungent odor reached me. "More practically, it will season the chicken we are having for dinner! And long ago, when herbs were used medicinally, it was good for . . . now, what was it good for?" She frowned making a furrow, the only line in a pretty face. "Well, it doesn't matter, because now we have penicillin and—and acupuncture!" She laughed. "Welcome to Bois, Stephanie. I am Sister Julie, your counselor."

"Thank you. But—how did you know I was Stephanie?"

"My dear, by the time you are admitted to Bois, we know so much about you, we could recognize you in a dark alley on a moonless night. I know Stephanie Martin is almost fifteen, brunette, slender, and a budding artist, of course. Besides," she admitted sheepishly, "you're wearing the name tag we sent you."

We laughed together.

"It's so good to be here!" I said with a huge sigh.

"Well, child, you *are* here, and I'll take you to your room."

And this, I thought dramatically, is the beginning of life for me. I considered my past a grey blob, dull and uneventful. I had no family except my aunt, an indifferent guardian. "Good luck," she'd said to me when I left her house this morning. It had sounded more like "Good riddance." And at my last school, I had made no friends. It wasn't that I didn't like people, it was just that I spent all my afternoons sketching or painting.

"Why don't you visit a friend?" Aunt Louise would ask.

"I don't want to. Besides, no one invited me."

"And no one ever will! You certainly don't take after anyone in my family. Your cousin Kate had dozens of friends. Why, she . . ." And then began a tiring list of her married daughter's virtues.

I didn't really care that my aunt didn't like me. After my mother died, I had cared about only one thing, becoming an artist. If you want to be an artist, Bois is the kind of school you dream of. When after six years, you finish, you *are* an artist, with an established reputation simply because you are a Bois graduate. If the admissions committee had found applicants more talented than I was, they had not come across any more determined, and they had awarded me a full scholarship, one of two for needy students. I didn't really have an outside opinion on my talent. I had stopped showing Aunt Louise what I drew after she said of a self-portrait, "Is that supposed to be you?"

Sister Julie, chatting cheerfully, led me into the convent just as the first drops of rain fell, accompanied by lightning and a roll of thunder so loud, it seemed to shake the earth. We climbed the wooden staircase, worn wavy by the footsteps of generations of girls, and walked along a dark hall lined with identical doors.

The Chalk Cross

"This is your room," said Sister Julie, opening one. "It does look austere," she added quickly, reading my thoughts. "The rooms were built for the nuns, you know. Cells, really. Students in the early days slept in a dormitory that we use now for drawing classes. The light is good *there*. But then they were downstairs and didn't have the pleasure of rain on the roof!" Sister Julie was almost shouting to make herself heard above the pounding rain.

"It looks . . . ," I said loudly, trying to think of something nice, but the room was so uninviting and the light so dim from one tiny dormer window, that I couldn't think of anything except that it didn't matter, and that sounded too much like something I might say to my aunt.

"You'll get so used to it, you won't even notice," Sister Julie said. "Besides, you'll only sleep here, and there's so much to do, and the bed is comfortable. New mattress. The only new thing around here!

"I'll leave you to unpack and change." Sister Julie stepped into the hall, turned, and added, "only new girls are coming this week; the old ones start Monday. When you hear the bell—Sister Felicity rings it—come down the stairs and down the hall. The room on the right is the meeting hall, the old parlor."

It doesn't take long to unpack one suitcase of underwear. Bois requires and furnishes uniforms, and I saw mine hanging in the closet—white blouses and plaid skirts. The uniforms are worn by students, then handed down and worn by others until they are faded and patched. But I'd seen Bois students on the street, and their pride lent them style. I put on my uniform, noticing the skillful mending of a small tear near the hem.

It would be no new experience for me to wear old things. Until now, my aunt had dressed me in clothes long ago outgrown by Kate. Nothing ever fitted, for my cousin had been fat, and her dresses hung on me lopsided. Once I'd tried to remodel a smocked calico I liked. I had taken it all apart and sewn new seams. "Loving hands at home," I'd heard a girl murmur, thus ending my venture into fashion.

Art materials were also furnished at Bois. I found mine on my desk by the window: a canvas knapsack containing a folding stool, two soft-lead pencils (no erasers), a drawing board with a clip, and lots of cheap white paper.

Sister Felicity's bell rang out, loud and deep like the plantation bells used long ago to summon slaves from the fields. Doors opened and forty girls dressed in identical uniforms and self-conscious expressions crowded the creaking staircase and pressed past Sister Felicity, who was energetically waving a big brass bell.

The long parlor, lined on one side with tall casement windows, had a fireplace at one end and a platform at the other. Chairs creaked and scraped as we settled down, trying to catch a glimpse of each other without seeming to. After a short time, the room was silent. The rain had stopped as suddenly as it had started. It was so quiet, I could hear drops falling off the roof outside, and the sun was already drawing heat from the earth in little clouds of steam.

Mother Marie-Thérèse, the mother superior, regally ancient, swept into the parlor, mounted the platform, and turned toward us. How many times had she looked out at forty new faces? She seemed to be counting those times. If I breathed she would hear me.

"There is only one Académie!" The voice came across time. I had never heard the school called anything but Bois. "It is a school demanding complete dedication from its students." She paused after each clipped sentence, taking a deep breath before the next. "You are here because we believe you have talent and will give that dedication necessary to develop the talent. If you cannot, you must leave. If you remain, in six years you will be artists and educated women."

My thoughts jumped ahead to that day and I saw myself standing modestly by my prize-winning painting. I must make it! It would be difficult and require everything I could possibly give, but I would do it.

Mother Marie-Thérèse was saying, "In 1743, les Dames de St. Geneviève, a French order devoted to educating girls, founded in New Orleans, l'Académie aux Bois, a boarding school for girls—orphans, Indians, free blacks, daughters of the newly founded city. L'Académie prospered, playing a leading role in the development of New Orleans. In 1880, the Dames altered the name to l'Académie aux Bois, Collège des Beaux Arts de la Nouvelle Orléans, and it became the school you now know, devoted entirely to the education of women artists. In this day of change, l'Académie remains as it has been, neither old-fashioned nor innovative for the sake of so-called progress. In our inflexible uniqueness lies our strength." Another long pause, giving us time to examine *that* thought. "Welcome to Bois."

It was a chilly welcome, deliberately designed to challenge us and proclaim Bois standards and tradition. I could feel its impact in the room.

The rest of the day was spent getting to know the school, each other, and the teachers. I did not try to make friends. I was used to being alone.

"Cheery rooms," one girl said to me, "for prisoners, that is!"

I knew the feeble joke was an attempt to be friendly. "Um," I answered.

We were shown the classrooms, the library, and the archives, rich in history of New Orleans. We met teachers, both nuns and laymen, and we were given books and our first assignment to be done outside class hours.

"What I want from you, my dear young ladies," began Mr. Dupuy, Bois's French drawing teacher, indicating by his tone that we were neither dear nor did he expect to get whatever it was he wanted. "What I want from you is ten pencil drawings, no more, no less, ten precisely. In black and white. I repeat—black and white," he spelled the two words. "The drawings will have a theme, a unifying subject. You may choose the theme." He graciously bestowed that privilege. "It will also be the theme of your 5,000-word essay to be assigned and approved by Sister Julie. You have four weeks to complete your drawings and four more for your essay. Ten drawings. Black and white. Pencil." Mr. Dupuy sighed deeply and in a resigned voice asked, "Any questions?"

One girl raised her hand.

The Chalk Cross

"Mr. Dupuy, Miss Sally, she was my art teacher before I came here, she said I have a good eye for color. Could I use just a teeny bit of water color? It would . . ."

"No color."

"No color at *all*? Don't you like color?"

Mr. Dupuy turned a frightening shade of red. "I *detest* color!" he shouted. "Color is the hiding place for a coward who cannot draw! King's raiments to disguise the peasant. NO COLOR!" He spluttered and subsided in a visible effort at control. "Ladies, you will express yourselves in black and white. When you are irresistibly drawn to color, *think* it in. Then you will have a full color painting." He stomped to the door, turned and yelled, "IN BLACK AND WHITE!" The door slammed on Mr. Dupuy.

In a relaxed way, none the less demanding for her mildness, Sister Julie told us about the essay. "Choose a subject that appeals to you," she said. "Something you care about or want to know about. The library at Bois is excellent and the archives unsurpassed in the city. Use them!"

I spent the next afternoon in the library and chose for my subject, "New Orleans: The Place and the People," a title borrowed from an early New Orleans writer, Grace King. It was a subject that interested me, that I had thought of before. I often sketched old houses, people too, dressed in period costume. Sister Julie approved and suggested I limit myself to a decade. I picked the 1830s, a time when New Orleans was just past its first century, already a fascinating jumble of diverse people, cultures, and religions, predominately French Catholic with a subculture of black voodooism, a city to match Bois in its uniqueness.

In the archives, I found firsthand accounts of epidemics, architects' renderings of early constructions, and journals kept by visiting Europeans. There was a newspaper of the time on film and a machine to project it. I went to bed so excited and keyed up over my project that it took me over an hour to fall asleep and I had one of those dreams that seems to go on all night. In the dream, I walked the narrow streets of old New Orleans, looking for something. Sister Felicity's bell waked me before I found it.

At early Mass, which was obligatory for Catholics like myself, I still had not calmed down. The chapel made me think of Mother Marie-Thérèse, pristine and elegant. Perhaps you grew to look like this place if you stayed long enough! The only ornament left in the chapel since the Church had stripped its interiors of pre-Vatican I frivolities was a cross suspended over the altar from the vaulted ceiling. On the cross hung a realistically suffering Christ in enameled wood, old and probably Spanish, I thought. I knelt in the first pew and stared at it. The incense used at benediction thickened in a fog around me. I coughed and choked, and as I gasped for air, the cross shimmered and blazed red. Just before I keeled over, I had time to realize I was fainting for the first time in my life.

The Cottage

"How are you feeling, Stephanie, dear?" asked Sister Julie bending over me. I was lying in my cot in my own cell-like room.

"I feel fine," I answered drowsily.

"Well, you just fainted magnificently. The best faint in years! We get at least one good faint at the beginning of each school year, you know. All that excitement and no breakfast. You'll settle down. Do you feel like breakfast?"

"Yes, please!" I said, getting out of bed. What a stupid thing I'd done. I didn't want the school thinking I couldn't keep up.

I went through the rest of the day normally, calm, almost detached. We had drawing for two and a half hours, an hour of English, then lunch, and afterwards, history, math, and science. Even math and science were art-oriented at Bois. We were going to learn how to grind our own pigments and apply them to a wooden panel with egg yolk, first having made a gesso ground for the wood. We would analyze the permanence of colors and study their visual and psychological effects. It was exactly the training I wanted.

At three-thirty, classes were over and we were free to work on our assignment. I left the convent alone. I was looking for a "Creole cottage," a "brick between posts," plastered, one-story house built by the French and popular in the early 1800s. The plan of a Creole cottage is square with two doors and two windows in front and a steep roof. It would be the subject of the first of my ten drawings.

I walked along St. Ann Street expecting to find a cottage directly on the street, and that is why I did not notice, at first, one set slightly back, with a low, wooden fence and a small garden in front. When I did see it, I knew it was what I wanted, almost as though my imagination had conjured it into being. It was definitely early 1800s, but it was amazingly well preserved and cared for, snowy white with a clump of banana trees shading its entrance. Perfect.

I unfolded my canvas stool on the opposite side of the street and sat down. I unpacked paper and a pencil from my knapsack and remembered unhappily Mr. Dupuy's reputation for detecting worked-over passages in a drawing, no matter how carefully disguised. "Relax," I told myself, but I felt tight. Pencil in hand, white paper staring up at me, I looked across the street. There were people on the steps I hadn't noticed before, a group of three children surrounding an old woman. They were part black, the old lady quite dark skinned and the three children coffee-and-cream colored. There was something strange about them, yet they looked just right for the house. That was it! They *were* just right! They were dressed in early nineteenth century costumes!

As I stared, they came into close focus, faces clear, voices audible. The old lady was speaking a foreign language, French it was, and I understood her.

"Sidonie, your mother wants only what is best for you," she was saying, and I found myself answering feelingly, "But I do not believe in Voodoo, Mère. I do not want to be queen like Maman. I want only to be an artist! I. . . ."

My voice faded out. I was sitting on my canvas stool staring at empty steps across the street. I felt completely disoriented, emotionally involved with the group of people that had disappeared. What had made me think the cottage was newly whitewashed? It was shabby-grey like the rest of the street with a part of the plaster sides fallen away, revealing the wood and brick underneath. I looked at my paper. I had drawn the old grandmother sitting with two girls and a little boy, all in nineteenth century dress. Through the door of the cottage I had shown a beautiful woman holding a snake.

Where had these people come from? Why had I drawn them when I meant to draw the cottage? Hardly any of it showed. My drawing was a portrait sketch, suitable for my project but alarmingly different from what I had set out to do. What had happened to me? Not more than twenty minutes had passed. The shadows on the porch had not lengthened.

I stood up, testing my knees. A little shaky. It was hot, and perspiration rolled down my neck. I remembered that I had fainted and been up late last night reading about the great epidemic of yellow fever in 1832 that claimed one out of six lives in New Orleans. That was it. I was overexcited. I walked gingerly back to school, knowing even then that heat and excitement could not explain everything.

That night, I slept fitfully, dreaming vivid, fragmented scenes of a half-remembered world in another time: There were two of us then—two little girls—and the city stank of plague. No. That was later. First, it smelled of sweet olive where we lived, where I am today, but changed, changed, and I must search through the narrow streets to find the places I once knew.

The cemetery is still here with its funny, not funny really, terrible little white houses for the dead because it is too swampy to bury underground. The bodies would float away, they say.

There is one tomb-house, newly whitewashed blinding white, but the stone is crumbling under the paint and the everlasting wreath is faded grey. MARIE LAVEAU is written in the stone. That is a name I know and the cross drawn in red chalk on the tomb has a special meaning. It is a cry through the wall to the spirit inside and it says, "Help, help! I have a favor to ask through the tomb and the years, Voodoo Lady. Listen to me! I want, I want . . ."

They still want. They have always wanted, and when she was alive, she had the power to give them what they wanted. She was tall and straight and coffee-and-cream colored with dark eyes that knew what had gone before and what was to come. Gold rings hung heavy from her ears and her skirts were long and full and swung round when she walked. She looked a queen, which she was, for she was the most powerful woman in New Orleans. She was Maman and I am one of the little girls. . . .

When I awoke, I could not shake loose from the dream world and my mouth was dry. I didn't think I was getting sick, but I felt edgy and out of myself in a funny way. At breakfast, a mug of café au lait, coffee and milk heated together, made me feel a little better. For the first time in my life, I wished I had someone my age I could really talk to. I tried smiling at the girl who'd made the joke about the rooms, but she was too busy talking to her neighbor to notice me.

In Mr. Dupuy's class, we had a fleshy nude model to draw.

"The *bones*!" cried Mr. Dupuy, passionately. "Think of the bones!" Mr. Dupuy waved his pencil in excitement. "The human body is a skeleton, dressed in muscles, flesh, and *fat. Strip* the skeleton. Draw what is underneath!"

I wondered how Mr. Dupuy had lived so long at such expenditure of emotion. His ideas produced giggles, but they worked. Some of the class drawings were beginning to take on character. Mine lacked something. They looked flimsy, but I comforted myself with the thought that I'd soon improve, once I settled down.

After drawing came Sister Harriet's art history, in which it seemed that without art, history would have gone unrecorded; then lunch, more classes, and at last, at three-thirty, it was time again for projects.

I walked back to St. Ann Street, telling myself I was going back to make the drawing I had intended to do in the first place, but I walked along the side of the street where the cottage stood, looking for—I wasn't sure what I expected to find. The street was familiar. I had a strong sense of having been there before, not just yesterday, but at some other time. I tried to remember something just out of reach. The smell of rosemary was strong. Someone was making tea. Rosemary for remembrance, Sister Julie had said.

I heard someone call, "Sidonie!"

"Je viens," I answered, but I didn't want to come. I grabbed at a fence, but I was moving away toward another time—a time too certain for dreaming, yet slipping out of memory. I struggled to hang on to now. My hands closed on nothing, and I slipped all the way back into remembering.

I remember that our street smelled of the sweet olive that grew in the garden and hung over the fence. I remember too how the iron gate clanked when I walked through. . . . The brick walk felt moss-fuzzy under my feet, and banana leaves formed a shade umbrella over the steps. . . . The cottage door had squeaky hinges . . . like a mouse . . . like this! . . . The door is opening! . . . I am afraid to go in, but now has faded out and . . . I am home once more!

"Bonjour, Sidonie, chérie."

"Bonjour, Maman."

I slip past Maman into the house. It is dark because the shutters are closed to keep out the heat. At first I can hardly see, but I smell the clover-scented beeswax Maman uses to polish the furniture. My eyes grow accustomed to the dark and there in the corner, I see an old woman, white, kinky hair glowing round her pruney face. But under the wrinkles, I love her. She is my grandmother, my Mère. She was the Queen of the Voodoos before Maman, but now she only tells us stories of long ago in another country. She no longer has the Power.

"Bonjour, Mère."

She answers with a welcoming smile.

I tiptoe past the closed door where my little brother Denaud sleeps. There in the morning light is my pale-blue room just as I left it. Dédé, my sister, lies cool between the sheets of our big bed watching the sun punch its way through the shutters. Soon, in spite of the shutters, the steamy heat will seep into every corner of the house.

"Dédé, get up. It is Madame de Blanc day. Maman is putting on her apron now."

Maman earns our living as a hairdresser because our father is dead, and she has a special apron, starched and white, with pockets, each a different size, to hold her scissors, curling iron, lotions, and creams.

"I'm too sleepy. And anyhow, Madame de Blanc will look ugly no matter what Maman does."

It is true that Madame de Blanc has a fat, oily face, but Maman can make that fat face narrow with her basket-of-fruit-style coiffure: a plait high around the head with poufs on top and one tiny curl in front of each ear, all held stiff with Maman's pomatums of beef marrow and tung oil, scented deliciously with patchouli.

When the hair is ready, Maman smoothes a white paste over Madame's oily skin and lets it dry until it cracks. Then she washes the paste away with her special lotion and—voilà!—Madame de Blanc is transformed, the oily pores shut tight, the skin soft and pink. And while Maman works, Madame talks and talks and Maman listens, murmuring, "Mais oui, Madame" and "Bien sûr, Madame" to keep the stream flowing, and at the end of a week of hairdressing, Maman knows the secret hopes and hates of the rich aristocrats of New Orleans, useful information for the Voodoo queen.

"Dédé, you are lazy. I am going to wake Denaud and take him in the garden."

"Donie! Not the garden!" At last she is wide awake. . . . And I remember. . . . Ah, but how could I have forgotten Damballah? Now, I remember everything. It was Damballah who made it all happen—Damballah, the black snake that lived in a cage under the honeysuckle vine in our garden.

·❊[III]❊·

The Future Queen

One summer morning, Dédé, Denaud, and I were lighting leftover firecrackers in the garden. Denaud accidentally threw one close to where Damballah, the snake, slept, and it went off with a loud bang. For a minute, Damballah writhed so fiercely, I thought he was hurt, but Dédé said, "Look at him! He is all right—only angry at the noise." Denaud would not look but hid his face in Dédé's skirt while I talked soothingly to Damballah.

"Damballah, we are so sorry. You are so beautiful, great snake. Do not be angry."

"He is not beautiful!" cried Denaud, looking up. "He's slimy and ugly and . . ."

"Hush, Denaud," whispered Dédé, pale.

"Come, Damballah," I pleaded, offering him honey in a spoon. "See what we have for you." But Damballah remained curled in an unforgiving knot.

That night, Denaud had a fever and Maman was very upset. I helped her make a strong gris-gris of salt, saffron, and clay, which she rubbed on Denaud's hot forehead.

Then she fed Damballah palm honey mixed with wine and crooned to him in Voodoo:

> *"Eh! Eh! Bomba, hen, hen! Canga bafia té!*
> *Eh, yé, yé, Mamzelle Marie,*
> *Ya, yé, yé, li konin tou gris-gris,*
> *Li té kouri lekal avec vieux kokodril,*
> *Oh, ouai, yé Mamzelle Marie. . . .*

Dédé tossed on her bed, halfway between sleep and waking, moaning, "I hate him! I hate Damballah!"

And I whispered, "Dédé, dear, don't say that! Damballah is listening!"

In the morning, Denaud was dancing about the house, pinching me and laughing when I pretended to cry, but Dédé had deep circles under her eyes and she refused the breakfast Mère made for her. Maman was very tired from nursing Denaud and comforting Damballah, but she gathered us around her and said, "Mes chers, you must never, *never* make Damballah angry. It is he who tells Maman what to do. He understands the long-ago past and sees the future, and he has great Power. What would we do without him? Free, yet black, neither aristocrats nor slaves. It is he who gives us our place in the world. And it is a position of power! Never forget that!"

"I have done nothing, Maman," Dédé said quietly.

Damballah had never liked Dédé. She had always stayed out of his way as much as possible, and if she had to go near the cage, she smiled. But after the firecracker incident, whenever she was close to him, he became excited and wriggled unpleasantly, flicking out his forked tongue.

The Chalk Cross

Maman said, "It is not that he does not like you, Dédé, my darling; it is only that he must make it absolutely clear who the Queen must be." She smiled at me and Damballah shook crazily and hissed at Dédé.

Later that same morning, Zouzou passed by on her way to the market. Zouzou was what Maman called a Voodoo meddler, someone who did not really have the Power, but pretended to. She hated Maman because Maman was beautiful while Zouzou looked like a small dog on spider legs. Once I had overheard Zouzou say, " 'Mamzelle the Queen' she calls herself! No better than the rest of us, I say. Don't all Voodoos have the Power?" Zouzou had a stall in the market where she sold herbs openly and worthless gris-gris secretly and tried with gossip and lies to persuade others that she had more Power than Maman.

As she strutted past our house that day, she suddenly spun around and caught Dédé sprinkling a salt cross in her footsteps to ward off evil. Her skinny spider-arms darted out and she dug her fingers into Dédé's wrist until Dédé winced and spilled the salt.

"You, daughter of the witch-queen," she snarled. "Take care the devil, Papa Le Bas, doesn't get you!"

Dédé went pale and before I could snatch Denaud away, he shouted in his high-pitched, little-boy voice, "Zouzou is a witch! Zouzou is a witch!"

"I know you, little son of the snake-queen!" screeched Zouzou, whirling around at him. "I know you, little neither-black-nor-white, little MULE!"

I pulled Denaud into the house, shaking him until his cheeks wobbled. "Zouzou is bad, Denaud, *bad*! You stay away from her or she'll do you some evil!"

"Zouzou is all wrinkly like a prune," said Denaud, pouting.

Dédé was sick with fright and went to bed for the rest of the day. Zouzou was so evil, I was glad that she did not have the Power as Maman had. But I did not want the Power either. I did not want people, rich white and slave black and all the shades between, sneaking to me with their hates and making me responsible. I did not want their troubles and I felt certain I could never help them. I had other plans for the future.

When I went to the priest, Père Antoine, for instruction, he told me I had a gift for drawing and that I learned quickly. "Such a gift is from God and should not be refused," he said.

I wanted to be an artist, but when I spoke of this to Maman, she said, "And what would you do? Design embroidery canvas? Teach? Women are not artists. Wait, Donie. You are so young, but you will see that I am right. I have told you Damballah knows the future. You are to be queen! Be ready tonight and perhaps you will begin to see."

"Not tonight! I am going to the levee to draw this evening," I answered. "There are so many faces, people who come from far away. . . ."

"Donie," Maman said sternly, "tonight, you will be with me."

After the heat of the day, the evening came in softly on a breeze. We opened the shutters to the cool night air. It was not damp and there was no danger of a miasma rising from the swamp. We sat on the steps outside with Mère while Maman moved around inside. I could always tell when Maman expected visitors. She became quiet and withdrawn. She was concentrating so that the Power could come into her.

"Mère," asked Dédé, "what am I?"

"You are a dear little girl, much loved by your grandmère."

"No, no, Mère," said Dédé. "I mean, Zouzou says I am neither black nor white, so what am I?"

"You are an octoroon," said Mère. "Your mother is a quadroon, and I am a mulatto."

"Why are you all something different?" asked Denaud. "I thought we were the same. I am a little boy," he added proudly, sticking out his chest, "and I am not a 'latto or a 'roon and when I am big I will be the captain of a ship!"

We could not help smiling although we did not want to discourage Denaud, and Mère went on to explain to Dédé, "I am part African, part Indian, and half white. The father of your mother was white, making your mother a quadroon, and your father was also white and that makes you children octoroons. That is the difference. Do you understand, mes enfants?"

"Where is our father?" asked Denaud, bored with the classifications of color.

"Dead," said Mère shortly.

"How did he die?" persisted Denaud, not realizing that Mère wanted to change the subject.

"He was killed in a duel. An affair of honor. And now, how would you like a story?"

"True or scary?" asked Denaud, immediately distracted.

"Which would you prefer?"

"True *and* scary!" cried Denaud, wiggling with delight.

"Well, now, cher, I think I recall a tale, terrible and

true, though it happened so long ago all in it are dead these many years."

"Begin now!" said Dédé, happy for the first time that day.

"Many years ago," Mère began, "there lived in the city a man who had everything. He was wellborn, with all the money anyone could spend in a lifetime. He loved his wife and was much loved by her. Only one thing failed. He had no children. For a while, he found happiness with his wife and the pleasures his wealth afforded, but finally it was not enough and he came to me for help, for in those days I had the Power. Yes, I said, I could help him find his heart's desire but there were conditions.

"First and easiest, his wife must drink a potion that I would prepare every night for twenty-eight days of each month for nine consecutive months. She must not forget even one single dose or I could promise nothing.

"Then, at the end of nine months, she must come to me. I would give her a doll to bring home and treat as a real child, offering it milk at feeding time and placing it in a cradle when she believed a real child might need sleep. They must try so hard to believe that the doll was real that they must omit nothing they would do in love and affection for their own child.

"Lastly, and perhaps most difficult, when the time came to christen the child, they must bring it to le Grand Zombi, whose secret church I would lead them to. If they did all this, I promised them, they would have their child. The man agreed but he had trouble persuading his wife for she was a devout Christian and found difficulty believing in Voodoo. However, her desire to please her husband and become a mother was stronger than her conscience and she did all that was required of her.

"The day of the christening arrived, and the couple drove up to my door in a magnificent carriage. In the arms of the wife lay the doll, dressed in a christening gown that had been in her family for three generations. I watched how fondly they handled the doll and I knew they had done their part. Night was approaching as I climbed into their carriage to lead them to the church of le Grand Zombi. The church lies far away from the city at the edge of the great lake, and the road that leads to it is so long and twisting that only the initiated can find the way. When we arrived, it was dark night, but the church, whose ceiling is an arch of oak limbs, was lighted by a full moon.

"Le Grand Zombi made his presence known, sending a breeze to rustle the hanging moss in the trees. The drums began, softly at first, and the Voodoos slid out from the woods into the clearing. They danced around the couple and the doll, chanting and beating the drums, 'Eh, yé, canga bafia té!' The drums beat louder and the dancing became wilder. The soft breeze became a wind, and clouds raced across the moon. The first drops of rain fell and lightning split the sky. I snatched the doll from the mother's arms and offered it up to le Grand Zombi. As the thunder cracked and the rain teemed down its baptism, I heard the faint mew of a newborn child and I placed it in its mother's arms. Swiftly, then, the three of us ran to the cover of the carriage as the storm roared about us.

"A bright flash of lightning lit up the darkness and I

looked at what lay in the arms of the mother. It was a black kitten! In horror, I waited for the mother to scream but her face held only love as she nestled the kitten closer. I could not believe my eyes when I watched the father gently lift the kitten from the mother's arms, and clasp it against his breast. The whole ride back I waited for one of them to shout the truth at me, but they only grew more enchanted and crooned lullabies to the kitten, who was indeed an unusually lovely animal.

"And do you know, mes enfants, that they raised that cat as their adored child? And when it died they grieved and held a funeral, and it is buried in the family tomb-house with an inscription on the stone that reads, 'Beloved, you are not forgotten!' "

By this time, Denaud was doubled up with laughter but Dédé poked him and said, "Denaud, you are a monster. That is a terrible, sad story. How can you possibly laugh? Would you laugh if Maman went crazy and if you were only a cat?" She turned to Mère. "Mère, it's not funny, is it? You said it was true; was it really true?"

"You did not like the story, Dédé?" asked Mère. For answer, Dédé burst into tears.

"It is fearsome, Mère," she sobbed. "Voodoo is fearsome!" She ran inside, past Maman who had come to the door to see what the commotion was about.

"And you, Donie," said Maman, who had heard the last. "Is Voodoo fearsome?"

"I like Mère's stories," I said, avoiding a direct answer.

"Come inside, Donie," said Maman. "I will have a caller tonight and I want you with me."

The Chalk Cross

I went in, first to Dédé. The room was dark and Dédé was in bed with her face to the wall, pretending to be asleep.

"Dédé, stop worrying about Voodoo."

"How can I stop worrying about it?" she answered miserably. "It's part of every day in this house. I hate it! I hate it when Maman talks to the snake. She turns into someone else and I don't know her. And all that magic! Why do we have to be so different from other people? Why does a cross drawn in red chalk bring power anyway?"

"You can't explain everything, Dédé. The magic's too old to understand, Mère says. But if it works, what difference does it make?"

"Donie, that sounds just like Maman! Sometimes I think you'll be queen just like Maman. Then you start drawing and I *know* Voodoo's wrong for you. You've got to fight it. Think of what Père Antoine would say."

"I do. And sometimes he seems to be saying the same things as Maman."

"Donie, he's not! You know he's not! And anyhow, you are an artist." She paused. "What's it like? How does it happen? Wanting to be an artist, I mean." Dédé fingered the blanket and waited for me to find the words.

"I reckon I was born with pictures tucked in my head, Dédé. Sometimes they form in back of my eyes while I'm looking at something. Then they just spill out on paper. Like Maman was born with the Power and has to use it."

"And Mère was born with stories. What was I born with, Donie?" Dédé looked at me wistfully.

"You were born to make people happy, Dédé," I said.

"You do, you know—like Père Antoine. Now, I've got to go to Maman. Don't worry, Dédé. I don't want to be queen, but I have to do what Maman says tonight."

Mère had put Denaud to bed and Maman was in the parlor, used only for visitors. The room was lit by a single candle on a table covered with a red cloth. Little spirit shadows flickered around Maman, sitting straight and beautiful in the middle of the room. I would have liked to draw her shadowed face with its high, Indian cheekbones and dark eyes of Africa, but there was something, some magic quality I knew I could not capture on paper. I looked at Mère, withered and yellow, and wondered if she had been beautiful when she had the Power. We waited. Soon we heard the wheels of a carriage on the cobblestones outside, and Mère shuffled from the room, leaving Maman and me in the parlor, which was no longer familiar.

·✤[IV]✤··

The Wax Doll

There was a light knock on the door.

"Entrez," said Maman, in her Mamzelle Laveau voice, rich as velvet.

The door opened and a heavily veiled woman slipped in.

"Bonsoir, Mamzelle," said the woman, nervously. She removed the veil, revealing the oily face of Madame de Blanc. So, Maman's transformation did not last long. "I have come to you for help," she said, too agitated to bother with polite preliminaries.

"Bien sûr, Madame. What can I do for you?" Maman's voice healed like balm.

"It is about Philomène!" she cried. Philomène was her daughter, as beautiful as the mother was ugly. "I believe her possessed. She thinks herself in love with Monsieur Ledoux—Philippe Ledoux, the apothecary, I mean. A shopkeeper!"

Madame de Blanc shook her head in disbelief at her own words. But I found it natural in Philomène to love Philippe, so handsome, especially when a smile deepened the corners of his mouth.

"Now she has locked herself in her room and says she threw away the key and will starve herself to death unless we allow her to marry that skinny, mealy, *penniless* worm!" Madame de Blanc had become so excited she spit when she said "penniless."

"Oui, Madame. Do not excite yourself. I understand. Possessed she must be, as those in love often are," said Maman dryly.

Madame de Blanc grew calmer. "I have heard that there are ways . . . I mean you are very clever . . . and I can pay!"

"Madame, of course, I understand. I have very potent gris-gris for affairs of the heart. But tell me, what will happen to your daughter if I prevent this marriage? Will she find happiness elsewhere?"

"Naturally, Mamzelle, we have plans, my husband and I. Philomène is to be married to the marquis." Madame de Blanc paused in expectation of Maman's astonishment, but Maman said nothing. Everyone knew Madame de Blanc had aristocratic connections and that her sister had married the owner of Belle Rose, the largest plantation in Louisiana. Madame de Blanc never lost an opportunity to remind her listeners of her importance.

Madame de Blanc continued, "I hope you can act quickly to prevent the marquis from learning of this disgraceful attachment. I am sure that once married to the marquis, an older, more suitable match, Philomène will be sensible—and quite sufficiently happy."

"Yes," Maman said thoughtfully and I knew she must be remembering the marquis's entrance into church last Sunday. He had passed close to us at the back, puffy-eyed, breath fetid from wine and rich food.

·31·

The Chalk Cross

"It will take a little time to find the proper ingredients, Madame, but the power in them is strong, and I feel certain of a favorable outcome. If you return tomorrow night I will be ready."

"Ah, Mamzelle Laveau," said Madame de Blanc with relief. "I knew I could rely on you. Your reputation for success in these matters is quite remarkable." She pressed a large coin into Maman's hand.

"Merci," murmured Maman, rising and guiding the woman out. When she had closed the door, Maman turned to me. "Quick, Donie, fetch Damballah."

"Maman! What are you going to do? Do not marry poor Philomène to that toad! She could never love him! She loves Philippe. He has beautiful, sad eyes and a lovely smile—and he gives me candy when I go into his shop. I am sure he must love Philomène very much. Maman, what will you do?"

"What is best."

"And who will decide what is best?"

"Do not be impertinent, Donie. I will know what is best. Now, fetch Damballah. First, I will consult him and you will see how it is done. You must not get involved, chérie. How would it be if I took to heart each and every situation that is brought to me? I would be dead of exhaustion in a month. No, we approach these things coolly, weighing the whole matter, and then it is clear what is to be done."

"Maman, I know what is to be done without consulting anyone. Help Philomène marry Philippe Ledoux!"

"Donie!"

The Wax Doll

I brought Damballah from the yard and put him on the table in the parlor. The detestable snake was writhing and hissing, but I dared not show I loathed him. Maman began to sing softly in Voodoo and as she sang, she swayed. Her earrings tinkled and her skirts swooped round like ripples in the water.

> *"Eh, yé, yé, Mamzelle Marie, ju suis,*
> *Ya, yé, yé, li konin tou gris-gris.*
> *Li konin bien li Grand Zombi,*
> *Oh, ouai, yé, Mamzelle Marie."*

Damballah stopped hissing and curved in rhythm to Maman's clanking earrings. Maman unfastened the cage door and Damballah wound himself around her arm. Maman was in a trance and stared into Damballah's eyes as she sang and swayed. Suddenly, Damballah jerked straight and it was as though a bolt of lightning shot from him into Maman's arm. The dance was over. Maman put Damballah back in his cage and turned calmly to me.

"Philomène will grow to love her marquis," she said. "Get the wax and we will make a doll for Madame de Blanc."

"Maman, I won't! I can't! The marquis is a fat lump and he smells like . . ."

"Immediately!"

When I returned with the wax, she had forgiven me and was smiling.

"Donie, chérie, if you want the gris-gris to work, you must not waste the Power out of you in a mad fit. You must channel it into the gris-gris. *Think* in the anger and hate. Think and will it into the 'ti doll, and there it will grow and fester and do its work like leaven in dough until the deed is done."

"Maman, it is wrong to hurt someone."

"Wrong? I would never do anything wrong. Is it wrong to do what is necessary so good can be accomplished?" Maman was indignant. "You have a lot of growing to do, Donie. But never mind," she patted my head. "You will do it, and then you will see."

I did not believe I would ever understand. "Do you think Philomène is really possessed?" I asked. "Could a spirit really inhabit a body?"

"But, of course, chérie! Does not Père Antoine tell you about the soul?"

"I do not mean a soul, Maman, I mean a spirit that does not belong in the body."

"I have known poor bodies possessed by dozens of spirits."

"Yes, but what about just one everyday spirit and the soul, each thinking different things?"

"Why not, Donie? When a body dies, the spirit must find another body or dwelling place of some sort, and it goes, maybe, into a body already occupied. It may also inhabit a tree or an animal, anything. There are spirits all around us, just as Père Antoine says."

"But, Maman, what Père Antoine says is not what you say."

"Mais oui! It is all true what the good Père Antoine is telling *and* what I am saying. It is only a different way of explaining the same thing. Père Antoine does not understand our way. It is very old and comes from a land

·34·

he does not know. But it is also true. I know. I believe it."

"Maman, believing will not make it so."

"Mais oui! If I did not believe, I would not have the Power, n'est-ce pas? And Père Antoine's faith—is it not belief in what he cannot *know* to be true?"

"Maman, how can I make you see what I mean?"

"Eh bien, Donie, and what is it *you* believe?"

"I believe what I see."

"*Everyone* believes what he sees. That is not belief. It is nothing!"

"Then I do not know what I believe."

"Ah, there it is. But do not worry, Donie, you will learn. Come," said Maman, losing interest. "We have a job to do."

We worked the wax until the heat from our fingers made it soft. Then Maman took a snake tooth and chicken feathers and a bit of dust from the graveyard and molded the wax around the mess. Next she formed a head, arms, and legs of wax. As Maman worked, she hummed a chant, and her long fingers seemed to bring the doll to life. When she was finished, she said, "Bonjour, Monsieur Ledoux," and laughed softly.

The next evening, I stood behind Maman when she gave the doll to Madame de Blanc.

"Voilà, Madame! Here is what you need. Listen carefully. At midnight, go to your window and in the light of the full moon, stick a pin deep into the head of this doll. Then hide the doll where no one will find it. From the head of the marquis, you must procure a lock of hair and . . ."

The Chalk Cross

"Alas, Mamzelle," Madame de Blanc interrupted, "the marquis is bald!"

"Ah, then from his favorite wig," Maman said impatiently, "and sew it into Philomène's pillow. Leave the doll hidden with the pin in it until Philomène unlocks her door and says the words, 'I renounce Philippe Ledoux. I am ready to marry the marquis.'"

That night I could not get to sleep. How could such foolishness change anything? Yet Maman believed, as did many many others, and I myself had seen Voodoo do its work. I could not disbelieve.

And was the church really different? In the chapel near our house, there was an altar especially built for a small, withered finger with a ruby ring on it, long ago detached from the hand of a holy woman. It rested alone on a bed of white satin, sealed in glass and framed ornately in gold leaf. All around the altar were discarded crutches and braces, left there by cripples who, in the presence of that finger, had said the miracle prayer, believed, and gone away whole.

Whose power rested on that satin pillow? Was it a power different from Damballah's? The Church would have nothing to do with Voodoo; we heard that often enough. Yet the same people crowding the church each Sunday came to Maman for help during the week. And Maman listened to Damballah and then spent hours praying in the cathedral.

It was Maman who was first to nurse the sick when the plagues came, she who comforted the prisoners in the Calaboose, the city jail. How often Père Antoine had knocked on the door at night, "Madame Laveau, it is

Celeste! Can you help?" Or "The prisoner is dying, Madame Laveau! Come quickly!" And Maman always went no matter how tired she was. It was confusing, different yet the same, and it bothered me when what I really wanted was to spend my time drawing and painting.

I liked the illustrations in Père Antoine's Bible, and I wanted to draw my own interpretations of stories. There was one picture of Christ, standing on a mountaintop with Satan crouched before him offering the world, represented by a tiny city of turrets, domes, and palm trees, but Christ looks cross and points to Satan to leave. I would have drawn Christ looking less sure of himself and Satan more attractive. Père Antoine says that Satan is very clever, so wouldn't Christ have been just a little tempted?

I would ask Père Antoine what he thought about it all in the morning when Dédé and I went for instruction.

·❦[V]❦··

Bois

"Good morning, Stephanie!"

"Dédé, it's too early," I mumbled.

"Day? Yes, it *is* day. And you've slept through Sister Felicity's bell," laughed Sister Julie. "And it *is* too early, but it's breakfast time just the same."

I sat up in a strange bed. I could not believe I was not in my own bed—my own bed? What was I thinking of? *This* was my own bed—here at Bois. I am Stephanie Martin! I made a deliberate effort to hold back panic and tried to remember. I remembered walking along St. Ann Street to the cottage and going in. I had entered another world—in a time past. I had lived the life of a girl called Sidonie Laveau who had no knowledge of Stephanie Martin.

"Breakfast in the parlor!" said Sister Julie at the door.

I reached for my portfolio. There was another drawing —a drawing I must have done, but I could not remember doing it. There was the cottage on St. Ann with Zouzou passing by and Dédé sprinkling salt in a cross on the walk. I knew these people. I was part of their life.

Sister Julie came into my room and stood watching me. "Is something wrong, Stephanie? Do you feel ill?"

"No, I'm fine. I just had a dream. . . . Sister Julie, that's not so. I didn't have a dream, it was *real*. This proves it!" My hand trembled as I handed her the drawing.

"What was real, Stephanie, dear?"

"I was someone else for a while and it was a long time ago. It was 1832—and it was real! I was a girl living then and my name was Donie—Sidonie Laveau." I could hear my voice going higher and higher, becoming less my own. I might turn into that other girl if I kept talking. I stopped and clung to myself, *Stephanie*!

Sister Julie was looking at my drawing. She spoke carefully. "Sometimes, dreams are very vivid, Stephanie, and you've just been reading about that time. Your name was—Donie? You are identifying with someone you read about because you are so impressionable. This drawing shows that." Sister Julie became confident. She was talking herself into a rational explanation. "The dream will fade as the day goes on. Come have some breakfast." She bent over me and gave my hand an encouraging tug.

I couldn't convince her that it had not been a dream. Maybe it was better that I couldn't. I didn't want Sister Julie to think something was wrong with me. *I* didn't want to think that either. I made myself stand up and say, "I'm coming." Sister Julie left, nodding approval.

Who were these people—Donie, Maman, Dédé—a whole world of them—and what had they to do with me? If I had lived another life with them, why was I remembering it now in this strange way? I did not want to be different. I wanted to be me, Stephanie, a girl studying to be an artist.

I dressed hurriedly, picked up my paper and pencils for drawing class, and left the room.

"Pencil, pencil, pencil!" sang Mr. Dupuy, as we drew. "Explore the marvelous pencil! Press down, lift up, look at *what* you're drawing, not *at* your drawing."

Suddenly he remembered to whom he was singing and changed to his most sarcastic tones. "My dear young ladies, did you know that once you could draw? Yes, indeed, it is no longer apparent, of course." He rattled yesterday's student efforts as though he held a handful of snakes. "But once, long ago, say when you were two or three, you were artists. Yes, artists. Then—then, you were 'taught art.' I see it all now. 'Stay within the line, dear! And, dear, grass is *green*, not purple!'" Color catapulted Mr. Dupuy into the present and a rage. "*Forget* color! *Forget* art teachers! DRAW!" He was gone.

The day passed quickly. After classes, one of the girls, her name was Annie something, asked me if I wanted to go to the drugstore for a malt.

"I'm going to the Cabildo to see the costumes," I answered shortly. I had not meant to be rude. I didn't even know how to go about being friendly to someone my age.

"It's too pretty a day to bury yourself in a museum," Annie said, trying again.

"I like museums. After the Cabildo, I'm going to the Presbytère," I answered, successfully ending both the conversation and the possibility of friendship. I had not meant to say that. I had not even thought about going to the museum until the words came out. Donie would have gone with Annie. She liked people, and for all the conflict between her and her mother, there was love too, and a real family life—something I had not known since my mother died.

I had moved into my aunt's house when my mother had gone to the hospital and I was just a little girl. My mother had said, "It will be like having a big sister, Stephanie. You'll share your cousin Kate's room until I come back."

Kate had welcomed me with the words, "Keep your flat clothes in your suitcase under the daybed. And don't hang much in the closet—my dresses will get squished. What's *that* stuff? Look at all those icky tubes of paint! You're not going to make a mess in my room, are you?"

"I can paint outside. And I'm just staying a little while. Until my mother is well." I had said this to comfort myself more than Kate.

But my mother hadn't gotten well, and I had stayed longer even than Kate, who married a boy Aunt Louise called "up and coming," and moved away. I had tried to cheer my aunt by painting for her a picture of Kate as a bride. "Thank you," she'd said, and later, absentmindedly used my picture to dump coffee grounds in. Those days, at least, were behind me!

I sighed, picked up my drawing things, and left for the Cabildo and the Presbytère, the two old buildings, now museums, that flank the cathedral.

Admission is free for Bois students, and my uniform was my pass. The first room of the Cabildo displayed Indian artifacts and wax figures dressed in colonial costumes, too early for my period. I hurried through, past maps and portraits of incredibly ugly colonials and examples of ornately carved colonial furniture, depressingly heavy. Something I remembered was waiting for me upstairs.

First, there was the big room with tall windows and high ceilings, where the Louisiana Purchase had been signed. A nagging at the back of my mind urged me on. I hung back, putting off going into the next room, forcing myself to imagine the colonial men of long ago, sitting around this very table, signing a paper that would vastly increase the size of the United States. But my delaying tactics didn't work, and I found myself at the door to the next room.

It was much darker and I had to wait for my eyes to adjust. The walls were hung with portraits. At the far end, there was a tremendous, greater-than-life-size picture of a monk. I moved toward it, staring into the dark-brown eyes of the familiar face. Père Antoine de Sedella stared back and drew me, stumbling, down the long room, past the wall of present time and into the world people call the past, where there was no Stephanie and I was someone else.

···⊰[VI]⊱···

Père Antoine

Père Antoine was really Spanish, sent to New Orleans when Louisiana belonged to Spain. He lived near the cathedral in a simple cottage. The floor of his tiny house was bare except for a few wooden planks he called his bed. In the middle of the room was a rough table and two stools. An ornately carved, enameled-wood cross with a suffering Jesus hung on the wall, contrasting with the room's simplicity.

"This crucifix comes from my home in Barcelona," Père Antoine told Dédé and me. "It is my reminder to humility. When I gaze on it, I remember that my Saviour died for me, a sinner." He smiled and added, "I also remember that because I keep this beautiful work of art, I am worldly."

No one thought Père Antoine was worldly, much less a sinner. He was believed to be a saint, a special friend of God's, and he was more loved than anyone in New Orleans. When he walked the streets in his coarse, brown cassock and sandaled feet, a wide straw hat shading his face in a checkerboard pattern, the people followed him, begging blessings and pressing food and money into his hands. Maman said he did not eat the food. He took it with him when he visited the poor and sick, and with the money, he bought medicine from Philippe Ledoux and gave everything away.

"Then he must be very hungry," said Denaud.

"He lives on bread and water," said Dédé. "You should try it, Denaud," she added, laughing and pinching his chubby bottom.

"And you should eat more! You are just skin and bones, Dédé. A wind would blow you away," said Denaud, quoting Mère.

"Let it try," Dédé said crossly. We were always after her to eat.

After breakfast, Dédé and I followed the familiar walk in the shadow of the cathedral to Père Antoine's and knocked at his door.

"Entrez!" he called.

"Bonjour, Père Antoine." Dédé and I curtsied carefully as Maman had taught us. "We have come for our lessons." I did not add that I had also come for advice, but one had the feeling that, like Maman, Père Antoine heard more than was said.

"I am happy to see you, my children. How is your dear maman?"

Père Antoine knew that Maman was the Voodoo queen, but he saw that in some strange way, she also accepted his faith, and he accepted her. How could I tell him that she believed in the power of a snake? I let Dédé murmur, "Very well, merci."

"I have something special for you today." Père Antoine

placed a roll of beautiful drawing paper on the table. "It was made in France, a gift of Captain Fontaine, whose ship docked yesterday. For you, Donie."

"Oh, thank you, Père Antoine!"

Such paper was too expensive for me to buy and I did most of my drawing with a pointed piece of red brick on coarse, brown paper.

"You will be a real artist someday, my child—if you care enough. And, now, let us begin."

Dédé and I sat on one stool, Père Antoine on the other. We began our sums. We used the black beads of his rosary to count on: one decade, plus one Our Father bead, minus half a decade. I liked sums and I liked to feel the beads, worn smooth by Père Antoine's long fingers. I was quick with the answers, but Dédé hated numbers and only answered when Père Antoine said to me, "Let Dédé answer this time."

After sums, we read from the Bible, combining reading with what Père Antoine called "a little meditation."

"Today, in our little meditation," he said, "we will use words spoken by God to the prophet Jeremiah: 'Am I a God when near and not one when far away? Can anyone hide in a dark corner without my seeing him? Do I not fill heaven and earth?'

"Perhaps, we have been thinking of God as a grey-bearded old man sitting on his throne in the sky, making rules and watching to see if we break them. 'Do this!' He commands, 'But do not do that or I will punish you forever.' But, no! He is really saying, 'Look Donie and Dédé, *this* is how I am. I am *here*—in this very room with you and Père Antoine. I am not only in heaven, I am everywhere!' He is joining us to his spirit, to the spirits of all who have ever lived so that the nearness of God is the nearness of all spirit. Do you understand what I am saying?"

"Yes, Père Antoine, I think so." But I was also thinking it sounds not unlike what Maman says. "You are saying that God is very close to us here?"

"Yes, yes, child, but I am also saying that if we allow Him, He *acts* through us. Do you see?"

I saw. I saw Maman was innocent because she believed she was doing the right thing, but that I must act because I knew what she had done to Philippe Ledoux and Philomène was wrong.

We said good-bye to Père Antoine and I gave my paper to Dédé to take home.

"Dédé," I said stiffly, "there's something I have to do." I did not want Dédé to know what I was thinking.

"Donie, if it's Voodoo meddling . . ."

"I am going to do what Père Antoine says I must. That should please you!" I said rudely, turning my back and walking away.

As soon as I was out of her sight, I began to run. Before I reached Philippe's door, I saw salt sprinkled in the shape of a cross, gleaming on the cobblestones in front of the shop. The shade was drawn and the door was locked. I was too late. Philippe Ledoux was dying, perhaps already dead.

The woman next door was sweeping her walk.

"Tell me, please," I said, "where is Monsieur Ledoux?"
She crossed herself. "I know nothing!"

"Please, please, Madame! Is he ill? I want to help him!"

"He needs help," she said, "but not your kind, daughter of the snake-queen." Her eyes went to the salt cross meant to ward off the Power of Voodoo. "Say an Ave for him for he lies in a coma in his room."

I had to save him! I would go to the de Blanc house and pull the pin out of the doll's head. Could I sneak into the courtyard through the carriage entrance? No, I would be seen by anyone in the house because all the rooms opened onto the courtyard garden. The front door on the street was closed to people like me, unless—yes!—that was it! Unless I was bringing something from Maman, some additional gris-gris!

I began walking rapidly. In my excitement, I almost tripped over a cat chewing on a chicken bone.

"Ah, 'ti chat," I said to the cat, "you have cleaned your bone very nicely, and now I will borrow it. Merci!"

I untied my tignon, the scarf that bound my hair, and wrapped it around the bone. I drew myself up into the proud posture of Maman's daughter, the future queen, and walked up to the de Blanc front door. I knocked. The door was opened by Angèle, Philomène's personal slave, her playmate when they were children and now her devoted servant. Everyone knew Angèle because she was beautiful and had extraordinary privileges for a slave. She knew who I was too, and made it clear from her look that I was not welcome.

In order to sound as disdainful as possible, she asked in English, instead of the usual French, "What do you want?"

I answered as proudly as she, "I have something for Madame de Blanc—Madame de Blanc, *personally*."

"Not at home." She started to close the door.

"No, Angèle, trust me!" I switched quickly to French. "I want to help Philomène!" Angèle's round eyes narrowed. "I must see *her*, Madame de Blanc, to help. Don't you believe me? Please, Angèle!"

She hesitated. "Wait." She left a crack in the door and disappeared into the house.

In a minute Madame de Blanc was there. "Yes, child? Come in, quickly."

Although many of the ladies of the city practiced Voodoo, either for amusement or because they wanted something, they did it secretly. Madame de Blanc did not want anyone to see the Voodoo queen's daughter at her door.

"What is it?" she asked nervously when I was inside.

"Maman sent me," I lied, "with gris-gris for you."

"But I need nothing more. The doll is doing its work."

"Oh, yes, but you see, I have something else that *is* needed. It is the little finger of a thirteen-year-old boy, taken from the graveyard at midnight." I stuck the bone close to her nose, and she drew back quickly. I wanted to laugh but I kept a straight face and continued. "You see, Madame, the doll has done its work and Monsieur Ledoux is in a coma." Madame de Blanc nodded nervously. "Now, to keep him in this state until Philomène has changed her mind about the marquis, we must channel in more power. See how no flesh clings to the bone?" Madame de Blanc shuddered. "So the flesh of Monsieur Ledoux must waste away!" I ended dramatically.

"But I do not want to murder him," Madame de Blanc stuttered.

"Naturally not, Madame! But we do not want him growing strong and rushing here to Philomène. Maybe even eloping with her!"

"Ah, mon Dieu, no! Quickly, let us do what must be done."

She led me down a hall where portraits of proud de Blancs glared down at the Voodoo queen's daughter. I followed her up a steep staircase and down another hall, wondering which of the closed doors was Philomène's. Madame de Blanc led the way into her own bedroom. I had never seen such a room. The bed was enormous, large enough for Dédé, Denaud, and me. It was made of a heavy, dark wood, ornately carved, and had a canopy supporting thick brocade curtains. The mosquito net was drawn back and there was a crocheted spread covering a wonderfully deep mattress. How Denaud would have bounced on it!

Angèle stood half-hidden behind the window curtains, hoping not to be noticed. I could tell she thought I had betrayed her and Philomène, and she was so intent on hating me that she made a hissing sound and drew Madame de Blanc's attention.

"Angèle," said Madame, "please go to the kitchen for Mademoiselle Philomène's gumbo and try to persuade her to eat."

Angèle left, not without another look of hate for me. Madame de Blanc said in her worried way, "Philomène still will not eat. Perhaps your Maman has a gris-gris for that too?"

"I will ask, Madame," I murmured.

We walked across the polished, wide floorboards to an

armoire that matched the bed in ponderous size and style. When Madame de Blanc opened the door, I saw at least twenty gowns hanging there. In one I saw a Paris label. All were of rich chiné silks or velvets and smelled of the spiced-rose-petal sachets that hung with them. But even with these dresses, she was not as beautiful as Maman in her calico.

Madame de Blanc looked around to make sure we were alone. Thrusting her hand deep into the dark armoire, she brought forth Philippe Ledoux made of wax. The heat had contorted him into an attitude of pain. I almost cried out when I saw the pin, driven deep into his head. How he must be suffering! My own head ached terribly, but trying to sound unconcerned and sure of myself, I said, "Maman says I am to pull out the pin and place the bone next to the doll in the hiding place."

"But your maman said to me quite clearly I should keep the doll hidden with the pin in its head until Philomène unlocks her door and says the words, 'I renounce Philippe Ledoux. I am ready to marry the marquis.' "

I have to admit I did not like spoiling Maman's gris-gris. I wanted to make Philippe Ledoux well and I wanted to do what I knew was right, but I was proud of Maman's reputation, and so I felt unhappy and frightened when I lied. "Ah, oui, Madame! But you see, it has taken Philomène a little longer to give in than Maman expected, and the Power in the pin is fading."

This had the desired effect on Madame de Blanc. I continued, "The bone of the little finger has just the right amount of Power to keep Monsieur Ledoux unconscious longer—without killing him, of course."

"I understand," said Madame de Blanc. "It was only that the pin was so successful. . . ."

"But not by tomorrow!"

"Yes, yes! Pull the pin!"

Carefully, I pulled the steel pin out, trying not to enlarge the holes it had already made. I worked the wax tenderly until the poor head was smooth again. Then, with a great show of useless gestures, I placed the chicken bone next to Philippe and thought in a little healing wish and a prayer to God for good measure, reminding Him that I was doing what I thought He wished of me and now it was up to Him. Making a soft bed out of my tignon for Philippe Ledoux and the chicken bone, I pushed them deep into the armoire.

"Voilà, Madame," I said imitating Maman's confidence. "It is done."

"Ah, merci, uh . . ." She did not know my name and I did not help her. If she gave me so much as a picayune, the smallest Spanish coin, I would accept it and buy Denaud a praline.

The coin was not forthcoming and Angèle appeared to show me out.

"Listen, Angèle," I whispered as soon as Madame de Blanc was out of earshot, "I am helping Philomène. Philippe Ledoux will get well. Tell her so and perhaps she will eat something and be strong when he comes to save her."

"Yes, I will. But it was your maman who made him ill. Why has she changed her mind?" Angèle spoke in French this time.

"She didn't mean to make him ill. Only to prevent the marriage. Anyhow, Maman does not know. *I* am doing this."

"You? But do *you* have the Power? I have never heard . . ."

"You will see," I said again. I let her believe I had the Power. It was not unpleasant to see admiration in her eyes. I left, confident I had saved Philippe Ledoux and that he and Philomène would soon be together.

There, I thought, I started out doing what Père Antoine said and ended up tangled in Voodoo. Where did one end and the other begin, and how could I choose between the two? I knew I must choose, for I was not like Maman. If I chose Voodoo and rejected God, I could not accept his gift. I did not like to think that, so I shut my mind to it.

As I passed in front of the cathedral, I heard the choir practicing. Up, up, up went their voices through the clouds and the floor of heaven.

·⊸[VII]⊷·

The Power

Through the cracks in the old floor, I could hear the voices of the nuns singing the Tantum Ergo in chapel. My portfolio lay in my lap. Without looking I knew there was a new drawing—another drawing I could not remember doing. I pulled it out. It was of Père Antoine counting the beads of his rosary with Dédé and Donie. I had drawn a cross on the wall behind him. It was the cross I had seen in his room, and the same one that was now hanging in the Bois chapel!

I tried to push back the fear I felt rising in me, and made myself look at facts. But what were the facts? Had I created Donie out of some need of my own? Or was I really Donie—dreaming about Stephanie? No, that was crazy! I was Stephanie. Crazy? *There* was a fact. I wasn't crazy. I was sure of that, because I was positive it was something *outside* me, and I knew what the something was. It was the Power. Only, instead of possessing it as Maman did, it possessed me, pulling me back into another time, then releasing me into now. Suppose I was pulled back and left, never to return, trapped forever in the wrong century? I must possess the Power as Maman did! That was it! If I were initiated with Donie . . . ? But I wasn't ready to go that far. I looked again at my drawing of Père Antoine, hoping to think of an easier solution.

In my drawing, Père Antoine looked much younger than in the Cabildo portrait, kinder too and more at peace with the world. It was a drawing of him through Donie's eyes. And through her hands?

I stayed close to school for the next few days. The old girls arrived bringing with them their self-importance and a lot of commotion, but the atmosphere of the archives remained remote from the bustle. I told myself I was doing research for my essay, but I was really hoping to discover a way to control the Power. I spent most of my time in the quiet stacks, thinking there must be something there.

In the old newspaper, *The Courier*, I read that Governor Claiborne had written to the Secretary of War:

We have a Spanish priest here who is a dangerous man: he rebelled against his superiors of his own church (at the time of the Inquisition) and was sent away . . . and I am inclined to think that I would be justified should I do likewise. This seditious priest is a Father Antonio; he is a great favorite of the Louisiana ladies; he has married many of them and christened all their children. [He'd married Maman and christened me and Dédé but I do not think Denaud was christened at all.] . . . He has influence with the people of color and, report says, embraces every opportunity to render them discontented with the American government.

And then again in *The Courier*:

The death of the venerable pastor who for fifty years was the support of the poor, the comforter of the afflicted, the example of toleration and piety, the death of such a man, we say, is a public calamity. . . . At his voice, the principles . . . of which his whole life was a constant practice did penetrate the soul and made everyone anxious to fulfill his duties.

Yes, that was my Père Antoine! Mine? Donie's! The more I read, the more confused I became, and I could find nothing about the Power. I wanted to talk to someone, someone my own age, but I had no friends and so I turned to Sister Julie.

"Sister Julie, who am I?"

"You are Stephanie Martin, a student artist working too hard!"

"Then, what about Donie? Where does she come in?"

"Do you think you're Donie as well?"

"Could I be?"

Another long pause. "Reincarnation, ghosts, things like that are not part of my faith," Sister Julie said dryly. "And I have rather a hard time with the mystics and miracles, I'm afraid. Take Christ feeding thousands with a few loaves of bread. I can't help but think there was a lot of psychology mixed up in that. You know, they wanted a miracle, so they pretended, even to themselves, that they'd had enough to eat. And maybe they really weren't hungry because they were so interested in this fantastic new teacher and what he had to say. Does that make sense?"

"Yes, it does," I couldn't help smiling, "to you. But you know, it's like Donie and her mother. They see things differently because they are different. For me, it's easier to believe that God simply worked a miracle! Why not, if He is God? Why go to the trouble of all that psychological hocus-pocus? But one or the other did happen, Sister Julie. I mean, either the miracle or the psychology. Well, with Donie and me, either it's some strange happening or—I'm sick in the head, isn't it? Sister Julie, I'm not sick—anywhere!"

"All right, Stephanie," said Sister Julie, "you are convincing. I don't think I believe in strange happenings yet, but I do believe in you. Get some sleep. You'll need it—leading two lives!" She smiled, made a motion between a thrown kiss and a blessing, and left me in my room.

But she did not believe in me enough because she told Mother Marie-Thérèse as I found out later and they worried over me.

"What you need is a change of scene," Sister Julie said the next day. "Too much of one thing. You are losing your perspective. Oh, I do not mean that in a drawing sense!" She chuckled at her accidental pun.

"Yes, but I can draw better if I'm steeped in the atmosphere of old New Orleans," I said.

"Then why don't you take the riverboat tour and visit a plantation or two for a day. That would get you out of the heat of the city but keep you in your precious period.

Oak Alley is lovely and the ruins of Belle Rose very romantic. . . ."

Sister Julie went on, describing plantations open to the public, but the name Belle Rose had touched the now familiar chord that tied my memory to another life, and back in my room I tried to remember what it was that made Belle Rose familiar . . . something Mère had said, wasn't it? No, it had to do with Philomène. If I could just remember without going back. . . . Yes, they had taken Philomène to Belle Rose and—and as I tried to remember why, I forgot to hang on to now. When I realized I was sliding back, it was too late. I reached out at nothing and found myself once again drawn into the tunnel whose other end opened into the year 1832.

·❦[VIII]❦·

The Journey

Mère had known a house slave at Belle Rose, and she often told us stories about Louisiana's finest plantation, owned by Madame de Blanc's brother-in-law, Charles Scott. Belle Rose produced more cotton than any of its neighbors, partly because it had more acres and more slaves, but mostly because its master from Pennsylvania was always trying out new ideas, usually with spectacular success. A Belle Rose slave took great pride in belonging to the best plantation in Louisiana. Once at market I'd heard a slave say, "I'm head cook on my plantation. I got four assistants." The other slave said, "That's nothing. I'm from Belle Rose." He was only a field hand, but the way he said it made them equal.

Mr. Scott was a widower, with one daughter, whose birth had carried away his wife, the sister of Madame de Blanc. It was soon after I'd been in the de Blanc house that Mr. Scott came to see Maman. They talked in the parlor a long time while I waited, afraid my chicken bone trick would be exposed. But finally the door opened and I heard Mr. Scott say to Maman, "Then, I can expect you within the week?"

"Oui, Mr. Scott, we will be there."

When he was gone, Maman said to me, "We are going to Belle Rose, Donie, you and I! Philomène is a stubborn case. She will not eat and she has not renounced the apothecary. They have moved her to Belle Rose but it has not helped." I tried to erase the guilty look I felt on my face. "We will go by riverboat, and we will have our own room in the great house when we get there. We will stay long enough to find out what ails Philomène, determine the cure and return. It will be a good experience for you, Donie, as well as a holiday. And when we return, we will have more money than we have ever had before!"

I had never been away from home, and Maman was looking at me expecting to see my pleasure. But I couldn't go! *She* mustn't go! She might find out about the chicken bone, and what would she do to me then?

"Donie?" I had waited too long.

"Maman, how can we leave? Denaud is so little and Mère needs me and Dédé and I must go to Père Antoine for instruction. . . ." I was ashamed at how I warmed to my own lie. There was Maman believing my lack of enthusiasm was unselfish!

"Ah, chère, we will arrange everything," she said, patting my arm. "You need not worry."

There was nothing more I could say. If Maman did not know about the chicken bone, maybe she could make Philomène well without ever learning. A trip by steamboat and our own room at Belle Rose was exciting enough to drive away fear of discovery and concern for Philomène. I would bring the drawing paper Père

Antoine had given me and draw all the things I saw for Dédé and Denaud to enjoy when I returned.

But something Maman had said still lodged uneasily in the back of my mind. "Determine the cure," she had said.

"Maman, you are not bringing Damballah!"

"And how could I accomplish anything without him?" she asked. "He will tell me what is wrong and give me the Power to make Philomène well. Of course we are bringing Damballah!"

"Then, I don't wish to go," I said, miserably. "Imagine what other people on the boat will think when they see a snake in a cage." I wanted to cry.

Maman, seeing my distress, said kindly, "We will cover the cage with my shawl, Donie, chérie. No one will guess it is Damballah. People will think we have a canary!"

"Yes, unless he hisses," I answered.

"Don't be ugly, Donie. It is difficult for me to leave. I have accepted this case for your sake." She looked at me anxiously and I gave in.

"All right, Maman, I'm sorry. I am glad we are going."

It took two days just to get ready. Mère would run the house as usual, but Dédé would have to market alone. Dédé was also sent around to postpone hair appointments, while I went to purchase a carpetbag to hold our things for the journey. Denaud was told over and over again all the things he was not allowed to do while Maman was absent.

"Walk only on the banquette unless Dédé is holding your hand. The horses tear through the streets, and the drivers do not pay attention to little boys who are not where they are supposed to be."

"Maman, I am big enough to cross the street alone!"

"You are not and you may not!"

Now was a moment I knew Maman wished our papa was with us.

"Don't worry, Maman," Dédé said quietly, and to Denaud, "Denaud, you little monkey, I will take you to the levee every day, but you must hold my hand crossing the street. Zouzou might get you if you don't!"

That did it. Denaud put his hand in Dédé's on the spot.

Maman asked around for the safest steamboat as carefully as she shopped for cloth to make a new dress. Not the *Enterprise*! Her captain, Henry Booth, had commanded the *Dispatch* when it ran into a hidden snag and sank in less than fifteen minutes, luckily, near enough to shore for its passengers to scramble to safety. Certainly not the *Maid of New Orleans*, for it was the second steamboat to bear that unfortunate name, the first having sunk with all passengers in a great ball of fire seconds after its boiler exploded. Perhaps the *Golden Eagle*? The ladies whose hair Maman set were consulted, and they checked with their husbands. Yes, the *Golden Eagle*. No one remembered anything unfavorable about Captain Caleb Wilkins. He was described to Maman as brave but not too daring. His boat was of the latest design, yet old enough to have stood the test of several voyages. Maman reserved two places on the *Golden Eagle*.

On the day we were to leave, the de Blancs sent their carriage to drive us to the boat. Dédé and Denaud were allowed to accompany us as far as the levee. This treat meant more to Denaud than the entire journey did to me. He was awake and dressed before the sun came up. The whole neighborhood knew where we were going though not exactly why, and everyone was out to wave au revoir, or as in the case of Zouzou, to peer with envy from behind parlor curtains.

"We are going to the *Golden Eagle!*" Denaud's voice was a full octave higher than normal and growing hoarse as he shouted the news to all.

Our elegant carriage rolled along St. Ann Street and into Royal. Wrought-iron balconies reached out over our heads, almost close enough to touch. Windows and doors were open to the lovely day, and I looked in at people going about their household tasks. We rolled past a tall black woman carrying a tray on her head. The tray was full of freshly baked brioches rolled in sugar. Maman saw me sniffing at them, ordered the driver to stop, and purchased one for each of us. She wanted so much for me to enjoy myself. And I was pleased with everything: the fresh morning, not yet heavy with heat or the dank odor of swamp miasma, the people walking briskly to work and market, shops with owners at the doors, waving greetings to Maman, and Maman smiling and bowing slightly at each greeting.

We arrived at the levee, a wall of earth fifteen feet high, thirty feet wide, and over one hundred miles long, built by slaves to keep the river from flooding the city. The levee was swarming with people: sailors, immigrants, visitors, foreigners, Indians, and residents of the city, for here was the heart of New Orleans, where its people came to buy, sell, and pass the time. It was all Dédé could do to keep Denaud from falling out of the carriage. Three-fourths of him hung out the window, and he was still shouting about the *Golden Eagle* and quite hoarse by the time he spotted his favorite boat, an ark. The arks were very long flatboats, made of timbers lashed together. They carried the produce of the Mississippi valley in one-way trips from Kentucky to New Orleans, where the cargo was sold and the boat broken up, its timbers used in buildings and sidewalks, leaving the Kentuckians to make their way home over land.

"Look at that ark!" croaked Denaud, laughing.

The captain was on deck, poling the flatboat along, and there, in an outlandish cabin, their faces framed by a curtained window, was the captain's wife and their milk cow!

"Moo-oo!" cried Denaud.

"Tais-toi!" said Maman, giving Denaud's bottom a light smack. "Don't be rude. Look for the *Golden Eagle*!"

Vendors were weaving among the crowd singing of the delicacies in the baskets carried on their heads, "Bon petit calas! Tout chaud! Pralines! Pecans!" Steamboats and sailing ships, anchored together in rows five deep, made a forest of masts and tall stacks. And there among them was the *Golden Eagle*! "Hurry, hurry," we were all saying at once, and "Good-bye, au revoir! Don't worry!" Denaud gazed in wonder, speechless at last.

The *Golden Eagle* stood out with her lacy, white wooden trim and bright golden eagle on the beam between the stacks. Passengers were hurrying aboard and the boat whistle was so loud and continuous I was afraid the vessel would leave before we could get on. But at last we were safe on board, our bag tucked under a bunk in the ladies' cabin, and Damballah hidden by Maman's shawl. We went up to the wide deck behind the wheelhouse and watched as we pulled away; first our little family, and then the cathedral towers, ducked behind the willow trees that lined the banks of the Mississippi beyond the city. The muddy current swirled in circles and rushed onward to the Gulf of Mexico, pushing against us as we toiled upriver, tooting and whistling at the flatboats.

We put in often at the small docks in front of each plantation to pick up firewood, fresh milk and provisions, and to exchange new passengers for old. I had never seen a plantation before and was amazed at the magnificent main houses. Huge, columned mansions surrounded by parks stood before fields of sugar cane and cotton.

I got out my paper and with a pointed piece of charcoal, I sketched a great white house gleaming through the dark trees. It was the first time I had ever drawn a building; I was used to drawing faces and paper dolls with a whole wardrobe of fashionable clothes, and it annoyed me to see that my plantation house looked wobbly instead of massive and sturdy. I thought too how nice it would have been if I had had some green color for the trees. Mère had shown me how to make color from weeds and wild flowers and I had a wide range of watercolors at home, but they were too bulky to travel with and I had to use shapes, dark shadows, and white spaces to take the place of color.

Maman and I ate our meal of bread baked by Mère and sausage, a present from one of Maman's ladies. Some families had servants traveling with them who prepared elaborate dinners in the boat's galley. Rich people like this, who would never have spoken to us on the street, were friendly and chatted to Maman and me. The boat somehow erased barriers and created a bond among its passengers. When I tried to do a portrait of Maman, a beautifully dressed girl, accompanied by her own slave, looked at it and said, "Why, that looks just like her!"

"Merci," I answered. I would have said more because I would have liked to know her, but I could not forget Damballah under the shawl. What would she think of a girl whose mother kept a snake?

We saw more mansions as we went along, one more beautiful than the next, but none of them prepared us for the splendor of Belle Rose. It was massive, yet graceful, with round, white columns nearly four feet in diameter rising from the ground to the roof, and porches upstairs and down encircling the house and shading windows left open to catch the breeze from the river. A long alley of oaks stretched from the dock to the wide entrance of the house, and in the back I saw pecan groves and cotton fields. Even if Mère had not told me, I would have known that Belle Rose stood alone among the plantations of Louisiana.

·•⊰[I X]⊱•··

Belle Rose

Mr. Scott himself waited on the dock with his daughter, and our fellow passengers watched with interest as we descended and were greeted by them.

A servant, the biggest man I had ever seen, well over six feet, smiled at me and took my bag.

"My name is Henri," said the giant black man. I had to look straight up to see his handsome face and return his smile. I answered with a shyness unusual to me, "I am Sidonie."

"I hope you will be happy here," said Marie Scott, so delicate and lovely, I felt clumsy next to her.

"Merci," I murmured, awed into stupidity by the atmosphere of Belle Rose and its splendid owners.

The entrance to the house was large enough for a carriage to roll through and led into a hall painted with a mural of life-size leopards, lions, and zebras in an African jungle. At the foot of wide steps curving upward, Mr. Scott turned to Maman and with a little bow, said, "Henri will show you to your room, Madame Laveau, and after you have rested, I will take you to Philomène.

My sister-in-law and her husband are so fatigued by the state of affairs that they pray you to excuse them."

Madame de Blanc here! The moment she saw me or Maman, she would talk about the chicken bone!

I glanced nervously at the shawl-covered cage Maman had not relinquished to Henri, and hoped fervently that Damballah would not hiss. He was absolutely quiet. I could feel him listening. Did he know about the chicken bone?

"Merci, Mr. Scott," said Maman, "but I will be ready immediately."

"Then my daughter, Marie, will take yours to see the fields while you are busy."

Henri took us to our room just to leave our bag. The room reminded me of Madame de Blanc's, only this one was less formal and decorated in a delicate pink just right for Marie. I stood at the open window and looked out over the levee to the swift-flowing river. What would it be like to be the daughter of this house?

Maman came up beside me and said, "Go with Marie and see the fields. There will be other times in the next few days when I will need you."

I sat with Marie Scott in an umbrella-shaded gig. She was polite enough, but I still felt awkward.

"I live in New Orleans in the winter," she said. "I board at l'Académie. Do you know the school?"

"Yes, I've heard of it." I could not say that Maman considered it too one-sidedly Roman Catholic for the future Voodoo queen; occasional instruction from Père Antoine who understood us was a better compromise.

Henri drove us into the cotton fields, which stretched

The Chalk Cross

as far as the eye could see. Large groups of field hands, one hundred in each group, mostly men, were picking the fiber from the plants in different parts of the fields.

"Henri is our lead man," Marie said, while Henri smiled proudly. "He is second to the overseer, and all the field hands are responsible to him. There are two hundred and fifty workers here at Belle Rose."

"Mr. Scott is a good master," said Henri. "He made a rule: you pick ten baskets a day and when you finish, you go fishing. Ten baskets are more than they do over at Uncle Sam plantation, where they have to pick till quitting time. We work fast—and then we go fishing!"

Both of them carefully avoided the word slave, and they did not seem to notice that all of Mr. Scott's goodness was ultimately good for the plantation as well as its workers.

We drove past small, identical houses. Children played happily on the porches. Would they still be happy when they were old enough to know what slavery meant?

"Each family gets five pounds of meat, one pack of meal, and a pint of syrup every Sunday," Marie said proudly.

"*And* there's corn pone, pot likker, bacon and sow belly, greens from the garden, and biscuits and molasses!" finished Henri. "Nobody goes hungry at Belle Rose. Howdy, Margaret!" Henri greeted a woman with children all around her, the smallest at her breast, the largest not much older than Denaud. "That's Margaret," said Henri. "Best mother in Louisiana. One baby every year! Don't do anything else. Don't *have* to!"

Marie blushed, "Some of our women are such good

mothers," she said primly, "that they take care of other children besides their own. You see, mothers can work until two weeks before their babies are born, and then we make them rest for two weeks afterwards. Most of those children you saw with Margaret belong, I'm sure, to other mothers."

She looked at me as though she expected me to say something but I could think of nothing that was not rude, and I was worrying over Maman seeing Madame de Blanc.

"You're tired," Marie said. "We'll go back so that you can rest before supper."

I was not tired but I was happy to leave the fields and go back to the pink and white bedroom. I opened the door pretending to myself that all that pink and white was my very own. I was just slipping into a fantasy where my hair hung in golden ringlets, when I heard a sound. I spun around, startled.

"Angèle, what are you doing?" She had been standing behind the door.

"No! What are *you* doing? About Philomène, I mean."

"I . . . I don't know! I didn't think I had to do anything. Maman will make her eat again, and didn't Philippe get well?" I asked uncertainly.

"Yes, he recovered suddenly, miraculously, he says, the day you pulled the pin from his head. And now I'll tell you what to do. Nothing! It is all right as it is," Angèle said, mysteriously happy. She knew a secret.

"But she doesn't eat yet, does she? That's not right!"

"She eats. Secretly. I feed her. She is not herself yet,

but we will take care of that. Just don't do anything except keep your mother away."

Angèle had a plan. I took a guess. "Is Philippe coming for her?"

Angèle could not keep silent. "Tonight! They will elope!"

"How wonderful!" I cried.

"Yes! I have packed everything. On the stroke of midnight, he will be under her window." Angèle smiled proudly, put her finger to her lips, and slipped out of the door, saying, "Just keep your mother away."

Oh, I would see to that! And I'd be awake, too, and from my window watch Philomène ride off on a horse with Philippe. An elopement! And *I* had made it possible. I had cured Philippe and saved Philomène.

Maman came in shortly after Angèle slipped away. She looked pale and baffled. My first thought was that Damballah had disgraced us. Mr. Scott, standing at the door, did not look unfriendly, and Maman was not angry. They had not discovered the bone.

"I am sorry, Mr. Scott," murmured Maman.

"Madame Laveau, you need more time. Do not distress yourself. You will succeed. It is the will of God."

"What happened, Maman?" I asked when Mr. Scott had left. I took her hand; she looked so distressed.

"I have never before failed so completely! I brought Damballah into the room. Philomène lay there white and smooth as the sheets. Only her large eyes and her poor thin fingers telling her rosary moved. Why has she not renounced the apothecary long ago? Immediately, Damballah began to hiss and writhe. The closer I came to the bed, the more Damballah misbehaved. Finally, I had to bring Damballah to our room and return to Philomène alone. Ah, she is ill! I could count slowly to ten between each of her shallow breaths."

I was becoming more and more uncomfortable. *I* did not have sure knowledge of God's will, and I was not certain I had done the right thing.

Maman continued, "I took Philomène's hand and she said to me, 'The Blessed Virgin is waiting for me in a rose garden in Heaven. I see the angels of God coming to take me to them.' 'No, no!' I said to her. 'You must stay with your mama and your lovely family a while longer.' I do not understand—this is *my* case and yet . . ."

Obviously it was only a question of time before Maman found me out. How could I have had the nerve to meddle in her Voodoo? And Philomène? Surely this was some act? Some pretense so no one would suspect the elopement?

"She continued to speak of her vision," said Maman. "I could not reach her with my words so I returned to Damballah for advice. He was curled into a tight knot in a corner of his cage. He would not come out when I crooned to him, even when I offered him honey. I have never seen him behave that way. I must talk to Madame de Blanc when she is fully rested."

That will do it, I thought. My trick will be found out and Maman will be furious.

Fortunately, Maman was so tired that I had little to do to keep my promise to Angèle. Soon after supper, Maman fed Damballah fresh honey from the plantation bees, and got into bed. I climbed in next to her, but of course I did not sleep. I was so excited I didn't even feel sleepy, and I was still wide awake at midnight.

The room was filled with moonlight and the scent of night-blooming jasmine. I crept to the window and looked out. I heard Damballah stir, but Maman was sound asleep. There, under the magnolia, I saw someone moving. Philippe! I heard his horse neigh softly. They were ready! Then suddenly, there was a commotion in the hall. Doors slammed. Voices. Someone running down the steps. The latch of the front door swung back with a clang. A shout, a shot, and a cry of despair heard above the sound of the horse galloping wildly away.

I stood rigid. Incredibly, Maman slept. Muted commands, urgent footsteps, and the house quieted once more. Maman had slept through it all! But Damballah was awake. I heard him hiss happily and I knew he was no longer curled in a knot. I climbed carefully into bed. It was dawn when I finally drifted off to sleep and noon when I was wakened by Maman coming into our room looking fresh and beautiful but very cold.

"It is done," she said smugly, "and just in time."

I knew by her look that she had found me out and that the elopement had failed.

"Donie, I do not want to say that what you did was wicked, and I am not so old that I have forgotten the romantic notions of love and youth. I understand that you thought you were doing the right thing. BUT—I will explain to you why you are wrong." All this was delivered in a tight, controlled voice. Maman was deeply angry.

"I will not dwell on the fact that if you had succeeded,

my reputation would have been shattered, and our livelihood—yours, Dédé's, Denaud's, Mère's, and mine—ruined. I will also not linger over your blatant disobedience and deceit. I will merely say that you are not mature enough to understand the way of the world or judge values or decide what is best for another. . . ."

"Maman," I interrupted. "I will never be old enough to run someone else's life. It is not a question of age. It is a question of *rights*! It is not my business to interfere. . . ."

"You are correct," said Maman, icily. "It is not your business to interfere. It is mine. We are leaving. Pack your bag. I will inform Mr. Scott."

And with that, she swept from the room, and I realized that there would never be words to bridge the difference in our thinking. I went looking for Angèle and found her huddled in a corner of the kitchen, crying softly. Cook was spreading an ointment on her back.

"She been whipped!" said Cook, her eyes wide with the horror of it. "And she been whipped *good*!"

Angèle looked like a small child. Her thick hair, usually braided neatly around her head, hung about her tear-stained face.

"I'm afraid," she whimpered.

"What happened, Angèle?" I was crying too.

"We were ready," she whispered. "No one knew but Philippe and me. And . . . and YOU!" Suspicion crept into her voice.

"I told no one, Angèle! Believe me!"

She was too wrapped up in what had happened to pay attention to me. "I woke Philomène and she sat up and let me dress her. She never said a word but just looked straight ahead. Then, as I put her cape around her shoulders, she picked up her bag, turned from me, and walked like a sleepwalker into her parents' room. She put down her bag at their bedside and in a queer, strained voice, she said the words, 'I renounce Philippe Ledoux. I am ready to marry the marquis.' I tried to keep her from going into that room! I tried but it was like trying to turn a machine on tracks. She was strong—strong! Ah, Philomène, my friend, my sister!" Angèle broke down and then she opened her eyes wide and looked at me. *"Where were you?"*

Cook pushed a cup of rosemary tea at her. "Here, child, drink. It will soothe you."

"I did nothing," I stammered miserably. "Neither did Maman. She *could* not. She slept and . . ." And then I remembered! It was such a shock I felt faint. "Mon Dieu! My God!" I cried. "The *curl*! I forgot the curl!"

"What curl?" asked Angèle and Cook together.

"The curl from the wig of the marquis! It is sewn into Philomène's pillow. We must get it out. That's what made her do it. Quick! We must get the curl!"

"Too late," said Angèle. "The marriage contract with the marquis is being made. The bishop has been told. Even now, Madame is writing letters to Paris, everywhere, announcing the marriage, inviting friends and relatives, making arrangements for the reception. . . ."

"But with the curl gone, Philomène would love Philippe again."

"No," said Angèle sadly. "You have not seen her. She is changed, really changed. The spirit has gone out of her. And you do not know the power of Madame de Blanc. Even without the gris-gris, I believe she would have won." Angèle began to cry again. "I'm afraid," she whispered brokenly.

The spirit went out of *me*. It was all my fault. I had forgotten the curl. I had ruined Philomène and Philippe's happiness and caused Angèle to be beaten. I was miserable as I had never been before in my life.

Maman, Damballah, and I left Belle Rose in Mr. Scott's best carriage. Maman did not speak to me until we were sitting close together, bouncing over the rough river road.

"Now, chérie," she said, forgiving me at last, "it has all turned out for the best, and you have learned a lesson, n'est-ce pas?"

"Yes, Maman," I answered wearily, too spent and unhappy to argue or even try to figure out what the lesson was I had really learned.

·◦[X]◦·

The Choice

"Do you find the lessons difficult?" Sister Julie was asking.

"Yes—*NO!*" I cried, my head reeling. I was thinking: What is this woman talking about? And on top of that came the thought: Poor Philomène! It's no use trying to run someone else's life. First, Madame de Blanc, then Maman, then me, full of good intentions—but what is this? I am STEPHANIE MARTIN!

I was so confused, I didn't realize right away that Sister Julie had said, "Then, why is Mr. Dupuy dissatisfied? Don't you like to draw best of all?"

"He doesn't like my drawing?" I asked, still muddled.

"Well," said Sister Julie, "he thinks you could do better and wonders why you don't."

What he thinks, I realized, my head suddenly clear, is not why, but *if* I can do better. He is thinking I shouldn't be here at all. I have to convince him—I have to convince them all—that I *do* belong here—that I *am* an artist!

I have to stop going back. If I *try*, if I don't get so

involved in the research but stay objective about it all, I won't be swept away. I have to stop *caring* what happens to Donie and her friends. They aren't even real, those people; they're not here . . . that makes them not real, doesn't it? Maman said I must not waste the Power in little fits. . . . I must channel it in . . . I must . . . But Maman was talking to *Donie*!

I WILL NOT GO BACK! I'll get some café au lait and go for a walk. Coffee always makes me feel better.

Sister Julie had asked me another question and was waiting for an answer, but I hadn't heard the question.

"Sister Julie, I think I'll have a cup of coffee and maybe walk to the French market. I want to do a drawing of the market, and I need a cup of coffee to get me there."

"Yes, do that," said Sister Julie with transparent false cheer. "There's nothing a good cup of coffee won't cure."

I meant to leave my room right after Sister Julie went away. I meant to get a cup of coffee. I lingered only long enough to wonder what it was about coffee that reminded me of something else . . . and found myself sitting with Mère on the front steps, sipping café au lait and nibbling croissants.

"Would you like gumbo for supper, Donie?" she was asking.

"Oh, yes, Mère," I answered.

"Then when you go to market, buy a chicken, please, and some onions and garlic. And I am sorry to say, we have no more filé. You must buy it from Zouzou."

"Then I will stay home!" cried Dédé.

"No, go and enjoy yourselves. I have something for you so you need have no fear of Zouzou." Mère handed

·77·

The Chalk Cross

us each a little red flannel bag. "Wear these amulets—and, of course, the holy medals of Père Antoine."

"How can this do anything, Mère?" asked Dédé skeptically.

"I will tell you how," Mère answered in her story voice, and Denaud wriggled with anticipation. "And I will tell you in the very words of your great-great-grand-mother." Mère made her voice quaky and began:

"In the forest where I lived, big-leafed vines matted the ground and wound tall around the trees; reaching out to each other, they formed a ceiling so closely woven, the sun had to change itself into a thin shower of golden coins to warm the earth. Beasts padded softly on the jungle floor, roaring their hungers, and bright-colored birds sang songs in our own language. It was a time long before the white men came.

"I lived with my parents in a tree house with a ladder of vines pulled up at night, and that is how I knew when I awoke in the dark and saw an old woman bending over me, that she was no ordinary person, needing a ladder to climb, but a witch, flown into my room. She was so hideous, her face covered with hairy moles, that I pinched myself to make sure I was not having a nightmare. She laughed, or rather cackled, for witches do not know how to laugh, and jumped on my chest, chanting in a strange language, drawing the spirit out of me, turning me into a zombi, a walking, soulless body.

"I reached for my amulet to protect me, but her witch eyes could see in the dark, and she pounced on it first, piercing the monkey-skin covering with her clawlike fingernails. Red pepper flew out of the amulet and up the witch's long nose, making a fire behind her eyes. She blew out with a terrible honking sneeze so violent, it shook the house and woke my parents.

"In the confusion of 'what is it?' and 'where?', the witch vanished. I babbled my story as we looked in every corner, making sure the witch had not changed herself into a mouse. But she had been destroyed; there was nothing left except a small pile of black dust—either the ashes of the witch or the red pepper turned black by heat. I could not tell."

"And, now, mes enfants," said Mère in her own voice, "I have sewn a pinch of that very dust into each of these three amulets. Wear them and you will be protected from evil."

I put mine on the chain with my holy medal. Dédé did not want to hurt Mère's feelings, but she did not believe so she hid hers on her shelf in the armoire. She told me her holy medal would be angry if it were worn with Voodoo charms, and Denaud lost his later that same day when we played hide and seek on the levee by the market.

Our shopping expedition began with Denaud trying to balance the basket on his head.

"Calas! Calas! Tout chaud! Rice cakes! Rice cakes! Very hot!" he shouted, imitating the chant of the vendeurs. But he was not very musical, and the basket rolled off his head, almost into the open gutter.

"Come along, Monsieur le Vendeur," Dédé said, laughing and forgetting her fear of Zouzou.

We walked down Chartres Street and stopped in front of the window of Monsieur DeLeon, the dentist. We could never pass his place without watching the life-size wax head displayed there. It had a large mouth that opened mechanically, revealing two rows of very white, perfectly shaped teeth. It opened, closed, paused, and reopened—voilà!—no teeth, only the empty cave of a mouth with a bottomless throat behind! We watched it gape open a dozen times or more; Denaud, each time, opened and closed his own mouth. Then we dragged him away, past the cafés, already filled with cigar-smoking men, laughing and gossiping, playing faro and roulette, and sipping eau de sucre or spirits.

When we came to the fashionable shop of Madame Pulce, Dédé saw a lace bonnet in the window. "I will have it!" she said. "For church!"

"And I will make a dress of the pink, candy-striped silk. It matches my room at Belle Rose!"

"It does not match your room on St. Ann Street," said Denaud, bored with Madame Pulce's wares and eager to reach the pet shop, which had a monkey for sale. Denaud, of course, imitated the monkey, who imitated Denaud, and we laughed until tears came.

From the pet shop, Denaud raced to the levee and shouted back to us, "Look at that boat! It is sailing over my head!"

And it did look that way from the city side of the levee because the river was higher than the land.

The levee was crowded with barrels of wine and luxuries from France and hundreds of bales of cotton from the plantations. We played hide and seek among the cotton bales until Denaud became so excited, he gave away his hiding place shouting, "Look! Look at that one!" and raced along the levee until the ship he admired disappeared around the bend of the river.

The morning was about to become afternoon when we persuaded Denaud to leave the levee and come to market. The market building was long and open, a roof held up by a square, pillared arcade with stalls between the pillars where people sold vegetables, meat, fish, herbs, and— gris-gris, if you knew whom to ask. Zouzou was that person.

Maman said that Zouzou's gris-gris was fake, "dirt and feathers" gathered by Zouzou from the debris of the market after it closed, useless and without Power. But Zouzou was rumored to be very wealthy from her trade to the superstitious and gullible.

We chanted a jingle about Zouzou's gris-gris. "Wrap it in a rag, tie it with hair, one from a horse and one from a mare."

We bought the chicken and vegetables we needed, putting off going to Zouzou.

"Let's have chocolate first," said Denaud.

"No, after," said Dédé.

At Manette's stall, you could buy hot chocolate and a small cake for a picayune, and we always finished our shopping day there.

"Get the bad over first, Denaud," I said. "The chocolate will taste sweeter."

We walked to the end of the market where Zouzou had her stall, weaving our way between shoppers and vendors. Zouzou saw us coming and her eyes narrowed. Then she looked away and busied herself with a customer. The customer was Angèle and she was buying gris-gris! I saw her tuck a conjure ball in her apron pocket. She looked around and saw me.

"Angèle," I began.

"Cochon!" she spat out at me. "Pig! You and your witch-mother. You make only misery!"

She turned and ran, upsetting a woman carrying a basket of blackberries on her head. Denaud scrambled for the fruit but Dédé caught him and slapped his hand lightly. Zouzou was smiling wickedly.

"Ah, little children of the witch-queen, what can I do for you? Do you need thyme or bay leaf or a string of grasshoppers for the mockingbird? Or maybe some of what Angèle bought, since your Maman's magic is stronger than yours?" She looked straight at me.

"What do you mean?" I said.

"I have ways of knowing what you did. Now, it is Angèle who needs gris-gris, and she has no wish for chicken bones from the Laveau ladies." Zouzou cackled gleefully.

"Dédé," I said, pushing the market basket at her, "take Denaud to buy chocolate. I have to find Angèle."

I ran in the direction Angèle had taken, almost tripping over an old Indian woman holding a bowl of steaming gumbo and rice. I had to stop and apologize and I was afraid I had lost Angèle in the crowd. But there she was standing behind one of the big pillars of the market, drying her eyes and straightening her hair. I came up behind her, grabbed her arm so she wouldn't run, and started talking fast, pleading with her to believe me.

"Angèle, you are wrong about me! I did try! I tried so hard to help, but you see, I really don't have the

Power—yet. I have not been initiated and all I could do was try to undo what Maman had done. You believed me at Belle Rose. Please believe me now!"

"Yes, but now it is worse!"

"How worse?"

"I am to be *sold*!" she cried tragically. "I cannot go with Philomène when she marries because I helped plan the elopement, and—and they have decided to sell me! They would have given me ten more lashes but they want me to look good when I go to the auction. That way, I will bring more money." Outrage shook her voice. "When we came back to New Orleans, they locked me up. Cook let me out but I must go back."

"No, no! You must escape!"

"I must wait for Henri," she said, resolutely drying her eyes.

"Henri? Of Belle Rose?"

"Yes, we are going to be married. Then, Henri says, perhaps Mr. Scott will buy me."

What a fairy tale! Slaves were forbidden to marry slaves from other households without special permission, and Henri would never get permission to marry Angèle. It would not "set the right example" for the other slaves.

"He will never buy you!"

"Henri says Mr. Scott is good to his people. He will understand."

Most white people seemed to think slaves were as happy with one husband or wife as another, having no sensibilities. Even when married slaves were sold apart, their owners simply chose new husbands and wives for them.

"Mr. Scott will not understand," I said. "He cares only for his plantation, not his people. You must escape, and I will help. I will help you both escape!"

I did not ask Angèle how she felt about my help, which, so far, had brought only more misery for everyone. I made up my mind in a moment, without hesitation.

"You will see. This time I will not fail. I will have the Power!"

But Angèle was not listening. "I must hurry back before they miss me," she said and slipped into the crowd, leaving me standing there, my head full of plans.

If I were initiated into Voodoo, I would be like Maman. I could do what I wanted—what *I* thought right. Yes, to have the Power was a good thing. The ways of Père Antoine were slow and unsure. I would use the Power only for good, of course. I would help Angèle and Henri escape to freedom!

My mind made up, I walked past l'Académie, the school Marie Scott went to in winter. Through the gate, I could see the nuns' herb garden. Maman sometimes got her rosemary from the sisters. If they had known what she used it for, they would never have let her have it. They thought she wanted it to burn with juniper for incense in the sick room, but Maman said it had magical powers. She used it to preserve youth.

I knocked at the convent gate. I would bring Maman a bouquet of herbs and tell her I had made up my mind and was ready to be initiated. As the smiling nun came toward me, I smelled the piquant rosemary in her hand.

·◦•[XI]•◦··

The Cathedral

"You've been in my herb garden," Sister Julie said. "Your room smells of rosemary. Oh, and you've done two drawings—a nice sketch of a quadroon or mulatto woman—and here's Belle Rose, just as it must have looked one hundred and fifty years ago."

Sister Julie picked up the drawing on my desk. She knew very little about art and judged pictures for their story content alone.

"You've caught the atmosphere of a real working plantation—nothing gone with the wind about this. It looks lived in. That's a wonderful-looking black man. My, he's huge compared to those two little girls. Why did you make him so big? Is it a portrait of someone you saw?"

"Yes, it's Henri," I answered, too distraught to realize what I was saying.

"The caretaker?" Sister Julie asked. I should have noticed the suspicion in her voice.

"No, he's lead man on the plantation, in charge of all the field sl . . . ," I stopped, but I'd gone too far.

The Chalk Cross

"Stephanie, I want you to come with me to Mother Marie-Thérèse. Now, there's no cause for alarm, but this has gone on long enough, and I just think you and she should talk things over."

Oh, why had I been so careless? Mother Marie-Thérèse would think I was crazy or something and send me away, back to Aunt Louise.

"Don't worry," said Sister Julie, reading my fears. "She'll help you do what's best."

People always say that when they want to talk you into something you don't want to do. I remembered the superior's chilly welcoming talk. I did not want to meet her face to face, but I got up and, together, Sister Julie and I went to the office. On the way, we passed Annie, talking to another girl.

"Hey, Stephanie," she said, turning to me. "You like museums so much—I went yesterday to the one in City Park. Have you been?"

"No. It's too far."

"Well, we didn't go for the *museum*. We went for a picnic. But it rained and we had to go inside, and what I want to tell you is, there's a portrait in there on the second floor on the left, and it's the *image* of you. It's called *Marie Laveau's Daughter!*" She laughed. "You're not related are you?"

"No!"

"Well, you ought to see it. Maybe she's a little darker than you are, but the eyes and mouth are identical! Hi, Sister Julie!"

Sister Julie didn't answer. She was staring at me.

As we entered the office, Mother Marie-Thérèse put

down some papers. "Stephanie, how are you?" She meant more than the conventional opening. "Let us talk about you, my dear," she added, taking off her reading glasses. "Sister Julie has been telling me that perhaps you are working too hard and have become upset. . . ."

"No, no, Reverend Mother!" I cried. "I really am not sick at all! I feel fine and . . ."

"Now, Stephanie, I have not said you were ill. Neither Sister Julie nor I think that. But overworked, over-wrought? Perhaps needing a rest?"

"Oh, no! I don't want to rest. I don't need to! I want to stay more than ever. I remember what you said about discipline and dedication, and I know I can do the work, and I've changed too! I guess you think I'm pretty peculiar, no friends, I mean, but I want friends. I . . ."

"Stephanie, my dear, calm down. Tell me slowly what has happened, please."

I took a deep breath and plunged. My whole future rested on how I told my story—Donie's story. I told Mother Marie-Thérèse that there had once been a girl called Sidonie Laveau. I had even read about her. I told about her family and friends, about her wish to be an artist; and then I said that in some strange way, I was involved in her life, that I was so influenced by it, I didn't know anymore where Donie's life ended and my memory began.

"I know it sounds impossible, Reverend Mother. I don't know how it can be. I don't suppose you even believe it all, but—but, please, I don't want to leave Bois!"

Mother Marie-Thérèse had never taken her eyes from

my face. Now she spoke slowly, still looking at me, measuring.

"We'll have to see what it means, Stephanie," she said with emphasis on "means." "Maybe you are finding a missing part of yourself, maturing, I want to say, in an unusual way. I know you are very imaginative. Then too there's God. . . ."

I suppose in any other kind of school, the doctor would have been sent for, but unlike most people, nuns *really* believe in God, and Mother Marie-Thérèse continued amazingly. "We *say* God can do all things, but we are always looking for rational explanations for what we don't understand. We should realize that God *does* do things—absolutely outlandish things—if it suits His purpose. He is not an old man sitting on a throne in the sky. He . . ."

"The same thing! Père Antoine says the same thing! And Maman, she said it too, when I asked her . . ." My voice died in my throat.

Mother Marie-Thérèse was staring at me. Slowly, she looked down at her papers. "Stephanie, we will have to see. . . ."

"Oh, please, don't send me away! I'll try not to go back anymore. I'll . . ." But I was thinking, if I go back, I can be initiated just like Donie. Then, I'll have the Power. I'll draw better than anyone in the school. I can go back and forth in time when *I* decide to. I had gone full circle in my thinking.

"I am not going to send you away, Stephanie," Mother Marie-Thérèse said rather tentatively. I felt I was being put on probation. "Try to put your best efforts into your class drawings. Mr. Dupuy is difficult to please. . . . We want to do what is best for you, my dear." *That* phrase again. "And it would be helpful if it were not known among the students that one among them thinks she is harboring a spirit from 1832. We are coming up for evaluation and appropriation of funds from the archdiocese. The archbishop hardly believes in art, much less reincarnation," she said dryly. "It will take a great deal of persuasion to get our budget funds this year." I had become lost in the far greater worry of the future of Bois.

Sister Julie smilingly accompanied me to my room; her worries had been shifted to the shoulders of Mother Marie-Thérèse.

I tried to appear relieved too. "Thanks, Sister Julie," I said with false gaiety. When I was alone, I continued to worry about my class drawings and the ones in the portfolio I wasn't sure I'd done.

I had fallen into a kind of routine: first, I'd feel a kind of tug, an idea to draw a certain thing and a feeling that something I knew was just out of reach of my memory. As the feeling grew stronger, it pulled me in a certain direction, and when I got there, I was Donie. I would try to stay detached, not get so involved in my drawing that I lost my identity. I would choose my own moment to go back.

So, when the thought came to me that a drawing of the interior of the cathedral would be a good addition to my portfolio, I examined the idea carefully. Did I really need the drawing for my portfolio? Yes, the cathedral was an important landmark. It had been there in 1832, but the steeples had been a different shape. I hadn't seen any drawings of what the interior had looked like then. It would be fun to see if I could tell on my own which parts were old and what had been added later. It was certainly not an emotional subject, something that might throw me back before I was ready. I could safely draw the interior.

I took my knapsack and walked down Chartres to the St. Louis Cathedral. As I came in, I heard the choir practicing with the organ for Sunday Mass. The temperature must have been five degrees lower in the dim, high-ceilinged church. I stood at the back, listening. The choir was singing the Ave Maria; the full notes of the organ backed them up. A group of tourists crowded in. No, they were not tourists; they must be people attending a service, because they were looking for seats and they were dressed in their Sunday best. Oh, Lord, they were dressed in their nineteenth century Sunday best!

·❧[XII]❧··

The Initiation

Everyone of importance had come to the Cathedral for the marriage of Philomène. Planters from the country with their wives, children, and servants had crowded the hotels a week before the wedding, and now, dressed in the latest fashions, they waited for the ceremony to begin.

I stood in the back with the uninvited. More beautiful than ever, but as white and cold as the statue of the Virgin that stood on the side altar, Philomène walked down the aisle on the arm of her father. The bishop himself performed the ceremony with Père Antoine assisting and a choir of boys chanting the nuptial mass. An energetic altar boy, swinging the incense burner as though his life depended on overpowering the fragrance of the orange blossoms, sent clouds of vapors around the bridal pair. The marquis had a fit of coughing, but Philomène continued to kneel, straight and still like the zombi she had become—because I had forgotten the curl.

A curl with Power that could change lives and a queen who had that Power in her hands. . . . What was it like to be queen? I thought of all the problems people brought to Maman. Maman did not become involved in them. She kept herself from caring what happened to people. But I had cared about Philomène, and now I cared about Angèle. If I cared about them all, I would be the way Maman said, dead of exhaustion in a month. Yet if I felt nothing, I would be a different person and maybe no one would matter to me, not even my family.

And what about God's gift to me? How could I accept that, now that I was turning from the giver? Drawing and painting were a part of me even though I might not be able to do what I wanted with them.

But—if I were queen, I would have the Power, and all my worries would dwindle to nothing. It was as simple as that. How could I choose anything less than the Power, available to me, Sidonie Laveau, the future Queen of the Voodoos?

I looked around the church for Philippe Ledoux, but he was not present. His apothecary shop was closed and he had disappeared, no one knew where. The Power of the de Blancs did indeed rival Maman's. Angèle was not at the wedding either. She had already been turned over to the auctioneer for fear she might plan another escape for Philomène.

After the bridal pair left the cathedral, I made my way to Mr. Theophilus's slave pen, where Angèle was being held, awaiting the auction. The entrance to the pen was through a small building on Chartres, and you could go in only if you were interested in buying a slave. But there were numerous knotholes in the wooden fence surrounding the yard, and it was common practice to look through these for a few minutes' entertainment. The guards were lenient to onlookers who taunted the slaves and provided a bit of amusement in the guards' boring day.

I had played their game; I offered nuts to the people in the cage, talking loudly, acting the clown, until one day, Angèle had seen me. Since then, I visited her daily at a hole hidden on her side by an oleander bush. I knew that today she would want me to tell her about the wedding. When I got there, she was waiting, but it was not the wedding she wanted to talk about.

"Henri has been captured!" she whispered through the knothole. "The patty-rollers got him!" Patty-rollers were the men who patrolled the roads, looking for runaway slaves. "He was on his way to me without a pass, and they caught him and returned him to Belle Rose. Then when he explained it all to Mr. Scott, do you know what Mr. Scott said? 'Henri, you have shown a lack of gratitude for all that has been done for you. Although I hate to lose a valuable man, I am obliged to sell you in order to set an example for the others.' Ah," moaned Angèle miserably, "they will not even unchain him to walk around the pen. They are afraid of him because he is so big. But the auctioneer says that if he is docile, a buyer will in all probability purchase us together," she ended wistfully.

I knew that that would never happen. I must help them; they needed me.

"This time I *will* help," I whispered to Angèle, just before a guard sauntered over to see why I was not being more entertaining. "Very amusing," I said to him. "I hate to leave."

"I've seen you here before," he said suspiciously.

"Yes, they never fail to make me laugh." I walked away as casually as I could.

That evening, I waited for Maman to come home. I avoided Dédé. She would know just by looking at me what I was thinking. I prepared myself carefully, for one cannot take an initiation lightly. As I washed my face, I tried to imagine the water cleansing my mind of everything but the desire to please le Grand Zombi and make me worthy of the Power. I felt a singleness of purpose I had never experienced before; I was indeed ready.

"Maman," I said as soon as she walked through the door, "le Grand Zombi is calling me and I am ready to give myself. I want to be a Voodoo." I did not mention the Power or being queen someday.

Maman's tired face changed immediately. She smiled with deep pleasure, but her embrace was formal. In her eyes, I had grown up.

"Ah, chère, I have so hoped for this," she said. "I will tell Damballah this very evening." I felt a slight wave of revulsion at the thought of the snake. "He will give me the sign when le Grand Zombi decides the time. I knew you would see one day. Damballah will be filled with joy."

I wished Damballah had nothing to do with my initiation. I tried thinking of him as something besides a snake, but he remained a snake.

While I waited impatiently for le Grand Zombi to inform Maman that it was time for my initiation, life proceeded as usual. We ate, slept, and catered to Damballah, and Dédé and I continued to go to Père

Antoine for instruction. But I had no interest in the sums. Dédé, timidly, answered them all.

"Donie, do you feel ill?" Père Antoine asked.

"No, Père Antoine, I am fine." I could not concentrate on the lesson. What I had once found so interesting, now seemed dull and unimportant. I sat staring out of Père Antoine's small window.

After we had read from the Bible, Père Antoine said, "Let us meditate on the words written by St. Paul to the Corinthians, people who lived long ago but who had many of the problems we have today. St. Paul says to them, 'For visible things last only for a time and the invisible things are eternal.' "

There it is again, I thought, just what Maman might have said from the Voodoo. I did not hear Père Antoine as I followed my own thoughts. Could it be that the Power was the same in Voodoo as in the Church and only the ways of tapping it different?

Père Antoine was saying, "And so it does not matter if we are rich or poor, slave or free in this world. Our life here is but a moment in the light of eternity. But life goes on after death. The spirit remains what it has formed itself to be and is either united to God or cast away from Him forever."

Dédé had not missed a word.

"And will I really see God if I'm good?" she asked.

"Yes, yes, my child! Face to face. And He will say, 'Come here, Dédé, my daughter. Welcome to my house, your house for all eternity!'

"Of course," Père Antoine continued, "the better you are, the clearer you will perceive God. Sometimes we die before our sight is completely clear, so for a while God sends us to a place where our souls are cleansed of any remaining evil still clouding our vision of Him."

"Where is this place?" I asked.

"No one knows. It is called purgatory, but that is just a name for a place we don't know much about." He paused and added thoughtfully, "It could be anywhere."

"Père Antoine," I asked, "why is it that the Church teaches one thing and Voodoo another and yet—yet, in some ways, they are alike?"

Dédé gasped at my impertinence, but Père Antoine answered, "Donie, mon enfant, God the father has many faces. He has made so many people and they too are different yet alike, and in order that all of His children may understand Him, He shows a different face to different people. And so, the similarities we see between faiths are shadows of the same truth, the beauty and love of God."

Dédé had been watching me and she looked so shocked, I felt she had read my thoughts and knew she was looking at the future queen.

On the way home, she would not speak to me so I said, "Look, Dédé, I am going to be initiated, but it doesn't really mean anything. It's expected of me. It's a formality I have to go through, for Maman, but you know how I really feel."

She looked at me and smiled uncertainly. "I suppose so," she said.

It was decided by le Grand Zombi that I was to be initiated on St. John's Eve. Maman passed the word to the Voodoos of the city. She sang a song as she walked past the house on the corner. In the middle of the second verse, she sang the message in code. The cook who worked in that house suddenly found she needed something at the market, and on her way there she too sang. And Doctor John, who was not a doctor at all, but who had a horse and carriage for hire, sang as his carriage rolled along the cobbled streets. In this way, news of the meeting traveled from one end of the city to the other, and we did not have to use drums, another way of sending messages, but one that alerted the authorities to a Voodoo meeting.

Maman had made my dress of fifty red and white handkerchiefs sewn together and tied at the waist by a blue cord. She lent me her own red shawl with the deep fringe, and she washed my hair with the special egg shampoo she used on her ladies. When it was dry, I looped it and tucked it under my tignon the way I'd seen Maman do. I fastened gold rings in my pierced ears and slipped into the dress. I pinched my cheeks and spun round making my skirt ripple.

"You look the spitting image of Maman," cried Dédé.

"Then, I am ready!"

"Oh, Donie, I know you have to go through with it, but I hate it and I'm afraid! Stay in the circle when you dance, or it will not work."

"Don't worry, Dédé, I do not get dizzy like you."

Maman walked in. She too had on a red dress tied with a blue cord and her heavy hair was tied up in a tignon. Maman had Indian hair, straight and blue-black, perfect with her dusky skin.

Mère stood with Dédé and Denaud on the steps as

Maman, carrying Damballah's cage, and I walked down the brick path to Doctor John's carriage. I stepped in, conscious of my long dress and importance.

The night was warm and windy. Clouds blew across the white moon, and the moss hanging from the trees danced like small ghosts in the dark.

"I hope it won't rain," I said, suddenly timid with Maman.

"It will not rain," said Maman, remote but certain. To have the Power takes concentration and I knew Maman was already thinking of the evening ahead. I did not speak again.

We drove quickly to the edge of town, leaving the cobblestones and following a winding dirt road, known only to the Voodoos. Through the trees, I saw the moonlit waters of the bayou. We followed the banks until we reached a bridge formed by a fallen oak. The carriage stopped and we crossed the bayou by foot. A group of people, carrying lanterns and chanting, met us.

"Follow me," whispered Maman.

I walked in the shadow she made, trying to hold myself as proudly as she did. We reached a clearing in the woods lit by torches and crowded with people, mostly black. But I knew by the dress of some that under their heavy veils, their skins were milky pale; these were Creole ladies whose hair Maman set. There were many like us, mixed blood, "gens de couleur," or quadroons and mulattos as the whites called us—or, as Zouzou spitefully called us, "mules."

Drums beat a steady rhythm; Voodoos swayed and

chanted. As we approached, they made an aisle for Maman and Damballah. I followed, caught up in the rhythm of the drum. Maman stepped up onto a makeshift stage of wooden planks and put Damballah's cage on a table in the center. There was sudden silence. Maman turned slowly to face me. She was no longer Maman. She was Marie Laveau, Queen of the Voodoos. She raised her arms high over me and closed her eyes. She began to chant:

> *L'Appé vini, le Grand Zombi,*
> *L'Appé vini pou fé gris-gris!*
> *Eh! Eh! Bomba, hen, hen!*
> *Canga bafia té, canga moune de le,*
> *Canga doki la,*
> *Canga li!*

The drums echoed the chant, and the people joined in the singing and swaying. I found myself alone, standing on a cross in a circle, all marked in the earth with red brick dust. The rhythm circled me round and claimed me. I was swaying and dancing with the rest, faster and faster. I was leading the rest, urging the drums on. My tignon flew off and my hair whipped round my head. The ground was the drum and I beat on it. Louder and faster, quicker and quicker!

Maman was coming toward me with Damballah and the Power. I saw it coming; I felt it reaching out at me. Maman extended her hand and touched my head. It was a shock that cast me out of my body, that body that could not stop whirling and went on wilder, wilder! As the drums closed in, I fell unconscious to the ground. The last thing I saw was the white moon exploding.

When I awoke, it was morning. Dédé was bending over me and I was in my bed.

"Are you all right, Donie? Do you feel different?" she asked anxiously.

"My head hurts," I said.

"Maman says you hit your head on a stone when you fell, but she says it is not a bad bruise."

I felt a small bump on the back of my head. "But did I stay in the circle?"

"Donie, Maman says it is not sure. She says the stone was just outside the circle, but it looked as though you fell inside with only your hair outside. Everyone believes you fell inside. Can't you tell? Don't you feel different?"

"I'm not sure. Last night when Maman touched me, I felt the Power, but now I just have a headache. Where is Maman?"

"She has gone to see Zouzou. *That* one! She is the only person who saw the stone outside the circle, and afterwards, she said to Maman, 'Perhaps le Grand Zombi is not sure of Sidonie, Mamzelle Laveau.'" Dédé imitated Zouzou's nasal voice. "Maman told me she is going to fix Zouzou once and for all before she has time to do more mischief."

"But, Dédé, maybe Zouzou is right and le Grand Zombi knows I do not really in my heart want the Power and is holding out. But still, last night, for a moment, I felt the Power and I *did* want it!"

"Donie, it is wrong for you. You will be an artist some day. We both know that."

"Oh, Dédé, I don't know what's right or wrong anymore! I only know my head hurts."

"I'm sorry, Donie. Rest," Dédé said.

I fell asleep and dreamed I was helping Maman change Zouzou into a little black dog with legs like a spider's.

·❖[XIII]❖·

The Portrait

There was a spider spinning a web in the corner of the window and the glare behind the web was giving me a headache. Mr. Dupuy pulled the filtering shade down, bathing the model we were drawing in warm pink. She stood on a block, straight and proud. So will Angèle look at the auction, I thought, and at the same time realized where I was—*who* I was!

"Stephanie Martin!" I said loudly.

The girl next to me turned and stared; I blushed and looked at the floor. Donie had been initiated. She was a Voodoo, the future queen. She had the Power. I tried to feel the Power within me. Had I been initiated? The girl next to me was still staring. I looked away at my easel. The drawing I had done of the model was flat, with no feeling in the line—"the bones were not there."

But in the portfolio at my feet, there was another drawing. I slipped it out and studied it. It was of Philomène's marriage in the cathedral. There were the well-dressed wedding guests, the zombi bride, and the fat marquis.

The Portrait

"Young lady, your drawing is *sterile!*" shouted Mr. Dupuy. He was standing behind me, looking at my easel and the drawing of the model. "All meaningless lines. Have you no feeling for what you are drawing? You are drawing a *person,* with intelligence, *life.* Not a paper doll!"

My face was scarlet with shame. His was the same color—but with indignation. Still shouting, he cried, "If you have no feeling for what you are drawing, you will never make an artist. *Never!*"

I stood up blind with tears, stuffed the drawings into my portfolio, tripped over the easel, sending it sprawling, and rushed from the room.

I had failed. Donie might have the Power, but I was as helpless as ever. I would be sent away from Bois, back to Aunt Louise. I would never draw again. I spent an hour in my gloomy room having imaginary conversations with Mr. Dupuy, in which I defended my drawings with clever arguments he could not refute. It was a glorious bath in self-pity and gave me a throbbing headache. But in my heart, I knew the drawings I had done in class were far below Bois standards.

Someone was knocking at my door. "Stephanie?"

The door opened as I tried to adjust my face to an I-could-care-less expression.

"The mean, hateful toad!" cried Annie, rushing in. "What a shabby way to treat anyone! He just wanted to be as mean as possible."

She picked up my portfolio and shuffled through the drawings.

"I like these," she said thoughtfully.

"What difference does it make?" I said rudely. "They want to send me away."

"Nonsense," said Annie. "Don't let them. Convince them you should stay. You're no worse than the rest of us, only—you *try* too hard. Maybe that's what makes your class drawings tight. Relax! Look, I know these," Annie held out the portfolio, "are better than the plant drawings I'm doing and no one's suggested *I* leave. Come on. Cheer up! You're going to be an *artist*."

"Thanks," I said. I was not going to admit that I wasn't sure who had done the drawings. I even managed a small smile.

"Now!" cried Annie suddenly. "You look even more like her! *Exactly* like her when you smile like that. You look just like the portrait of Marie Laveau's daughter. Come on. We're going to see it. Now! We'll take the bus and be back for supper."

"No. No, I can't go. I—I have a headache." I had a terrible fear of something connected with the portrait.

But Annie wouldn't give up.

"You've got to go," she said. "You've got to get away from here."

She pulled me up and we left. I felt like a zombi, totally outside myself until we walked through the gates of Bois. It was the first time since I'd come here that I'd really gotten away from my brooding self-interest. Annie talked the whole way out to City Park—pleasant, not very important observations about school and students. I found myself telling her how I felt about art, my aunt—things I'd never told anyone before.

"You know," said Annie, "you just can't work all the

time. A little fun might even put enough life into your drawings to satisfy Mr. Doo-phew."

The bus followed the curve of Bayou St. John, perhaps over the very spot that once was the secret Voodoo place. We got out at the entrance to the park. Annie skipped and half ran to the museum, calling me to hurry, anxious to see my reaction to the portrait. She bounded up the wide museum staircase two steps at a time. I had gradually slowed. What would I do if the portrait snapped me back to 1832—in front of Annie? Would I go into a trance or something crazy? It was too late to think about it. We had arrived. Donie's dark-brown eyes looked out of the portrait straight at me, pleading, asking something of me.

"Well? Well? Isn't it you?"

"I can't tell," I answered slowly and truthfully. I read the title, *Portrait of Marie Laveau's Daughter*. "It's Donie, all right, but I didn't think I looked like that. I didn't think I was that pretty!"

"What do you mean, 'It's Donie'? Who's Donie?"

"It's what she was called," I said. "It's short for Sidonie." I had to do better than that. "You know, that's my period for the project and I'm doing all this reading and research, and somewhere they describe her and say that Marie Laveau's daughter was called Donie, short for Sidonie."

"Oh," said Annie quietly. I did not lie convincingly. After a pause, she asked, "Didn't you know you were pretty?"

I blushed. "I'm not pretty! My aunt's told me a million times in a million ways how plain I am."

"Well, your aunt has poor taste or she's mean or something. You're pretty when you smile, and you ought to know it. Come on, if we hurry we can find the ice-cream man before we go back."

"Annie, I want to talk to you about something."

"Sure," she answered. "But let's go outside by the lagoon."

We found a shady spot under an oak, which we shared with a duck family, while I told Annie everything I'd told Mother Marie-Thérèse. I did not tell Annie my greatest fear was that I might go back in time never to return, but I admitted that I was afraid the portfolio drawings weren't mine. She listened without comment until I said that.

"Of course, they're yours," she said immediately. "You don't suppose a ghost did them, do you? With a ghost pencil? The only reason you don't *know* you did them is because you get so involved drawing them. All creativity is supposed to be like that. You start to draw or write, something takes over, and when you're finished, you wonder where it came from."

"Annie, you remind me of Dédé!"

"Dédé?"

"Donie's sister. She was a comforting person."

"Well, I'm glad. Let's get that ice cream before we have to go back."

But as I thought of Dédé, I remembered I had a headache, something to do with hitting my head on a stone. *NO!* No, that was *Donie.* Oh, please, not now! Not now when I am with Annie! I *fought.* "Annie!" I tried to call, but it came out, "Dédé!"

The Portrait

The ducks in the lagoon were swimming away, and I was no longer sitting in the park. I was in a lush garden of clinging vines and heavily scented flowers.

··❊[XIV]❊··

The Auction

The honeysuckle smelled oversweet in the sticky heat of the morning. Summer was reaching its climax and the only relief from the heat came at sundown and during the violent afternoon thundershowers. Crickets buzzed incessantly as I opened the door of Damballah's cage. His beady eyes were fixed on me, watching every move I made. He did not trust me, but he was quiet as I drew him out and held him high over my head.

There, on the grass, I danced to please him, singing the ancient Voodoo chant that told him he was great and begged for transference of the Power from him to me.

> *Eh, yé, canga bafia ten,*
> *Ya, yé, yé, li konin tou, gris-gris.*
> *Le konin bien li Grand Zombi!*
> *L'Appé vine pou fé mouri.*

As I danced, his body tightened around my arm. I could not take my eyes from his eyes. We went round and round together, and yes, I felt it coming: first a little wisp of knowledge, then a great flooding wave of knowing. I could do it! I could help Angèle and Henri. I knew how and I had the Power!

I went inside to make the gris-gris.

"What are you doing?"

It was Dédé. The weather was making my headache worse. I held my hand to my forehead and squinted at her through the pain.

"Nothing," I said. "I'm not doing anything." If I talked to her, the Power would seep out of me.

"You're meddling in Voodoo! I know you are. I saw you go outside to Damballah. Donie, how could you? You know Voodoo is bad—evil—and Damballah is a—a—Damballah is just a stupid snake!"

"Tais-toi, Dédé. Shut up, for God's sake. You are ruining everything and Damballah will fix you!"

"Damballah won't and can't. *I don't believe in him!*"

I slammed the door on Dédé. I had to make the gris-gris before the Power ebbed away altogether.

I uncorked a little bottle and, crooning all the time, channeling the Power, I mixed the ingredients:

> *Hair from a black cat,*
> *Cayenne pepper ground finer than dust,*
> *Seven red ants, shiny and fat,*
> *Pollen from nine blue buttercups,*
> *And a pinch of fresh-cut snuff.*

I poured them into the bottle, shook it well, and corked it tight. When I was finished, I held escape for Angèle and Henri in my hands!

The auction was to take place at noon. I went to the slave pen and put my eye to the hole in the fence surrounding it. Black bodies were crowded together, some standing straight and proud, others slumping in weary despair, mothers nursing infants, children staring at nothing, and chained, all chained together by their arms in lots of four. There, walking among them, his whip flicking like Damballah's tongue, was the auctioneer, the encanteur. He stopped at Henri, who towered over him, reached up and opened Henri's mouth. Standing on tiptoe he peered in. "Good teeth!" He felt Henri's muscular arm. "An ox! Should bring well over a thousand."

"Now, listen, all of you!" the auctioneer shouted. "Look your best when you go into the hall. Stand straight, walk briskly, and *smile.* A pleasant face means a docile disposition and a docile disposition means you'll be bought for the best jobs—pleasant work—cooking and sewing for the women, house work, and for you men, coach drivers, valets—no field work if you can show you have a skill and a cheerful disposition! Now, here are your clothes. Put them on."

He walked around unlocking the chains, whip ready. Chained slaves made people think of uprisings, and uprisings made buyers nervous. It had to appear that these slaves were content, happy, if possible.

The encanteur tossed a clean pile of garments to each slave. The clothes were of good quality, clean and colorful, part of the show, calico dresses, white aprons, and madras tignons for the women, and blue pantaloons, coats, white shirts, and even a few stovepipe hats for the men.

The whip flicked with a life of its own as its master said, "Get a move on, now! Get into those clothes!"

The Auction

The encanteur was the most famous in New Orleans. He knew how to get buyers excited and make them bid higher. He could make them laugh and enjoy themselves, and he knew how to make the slaves step lively and appear happy. His slaves were the best-looking, the healthiest and brought the most money, and his manner at the auction was like that of a showman on stage. And it was a show, one of the biggest shows in the city, rivaling both the theater and the opera. People came from all over the country, sometimes from foreign countries, to buy or just to watch. The auction was conducted in two languages, French and English, everything said twice.

I walked down Chartres Street to the St. Louis Hotel, where the sale was to be held. The slaves formed a parade through the streets from the pen to the hotel's great rotunda. They stepped to the music of a banjo played by Calabash, a black midget, a kind of clown, who was supposed to lend gaiety to the atmosphere.

The rotunda was like a palace with marble floors and a high-domed, white ceiling trimmed in gold. The auction platform was in the center, and there were rooms on the side for private inspection of wares. That meant a buyer could have a slave brought into one of the rooms, strip him and expose him to all sorts of indignities—and call it inspection of purchase. The slave was, after all, a piece of property, only more expensive than most of the other merchandise sold at auction.

People were milling about the hall, now thick with cigar smoke, waiting for the auction to begin. I did not want to be noticed, but I need not have worried; attention was turned to Calabash and the sound of the banjo. The encanteur came first, then the midget leading the parade of slaves, pathetic in their efforts to smile and keep step to the tune of "Jump Bullfrog."

Buyers stared intently. Angèle stood out because of her beauty and dignity. Henri too was exceptional, far larger than anyone in the hall, yet with an appealing gentleness in his strength.

"I need a cook," I heard one lady say, "and a seamstress."

"I am buying a hairdresser," said her friend. "With so many daughters, it will be an economy. When we are not using her, I will send her to others and charge them for her services. A good investment, n'est-ce pas?"

"Ah, oui! Madame Durand makes fifty a year with hers, and she can't even trim."

You could buy any kind of slave you wanted; you could even raise your own slaves if you got yourself a "breeder," a woman like Margaret of Belle Rose. For sale were carpenters, grooms, gourmet cooks—the list went on and on, the rarer the skill, the higher the price. But the highest price was paid for beautiful young women. Their use was determined by the buyer. Angèle would come under this category. She was not skilled in anything in particular, having spent her life almost as pampered as Philomène.

The parade was over, the auctioneer ready to begin, when a fat man next to me pushed his cigar to the side of his mouth and yelled, "That one!" nodding in the direction of Angèle. "Six hundred!"

"Seven fifty!" came from the other side.

"One moment, un moment, s'il vous plaît! One

moment, please!" cried the auctioneer, smirking. "This girl is special. No field hand here, and no breeder." He looked lewdly at Angèle's slender hips. The audience appreciated the joke.

"Bidding *begins* at one thousand!"

There was an air of excitement, and the same two men began again. Angèle looked at neither of them. She held her head high and stared at the wall. I watched Henri. The whites of his eyes flicked on one side then on the other as he followed the rapid bidding.

"Sold!" cried the auctioneer, jabbing his whip handle in the direction of the man next to me. "Sold for one thousand four hundred and fifty dollars!"

There were gasps and murmurs. It was a good price. The fat man pushed forward to claim his property.

"Bring her to the rooms," he shouted to the encanteur who motioned to a guard. Everyone in the hall was looking at Angèle.

"Now," I thought. "Now!"

I wove my way in and out among the people toward the auction block. I uncorked the bottle. The Power curled in a little wisp toward Henri. I watched the change come over him. He seemed to be having a convulsion as his gentleness was shorn away. At the same time, the Power caused the encanteur to have a sneezing fit, blinding him with tears and attracting the attention of the audience. Henri drew himself up, filled by a terrible strength, and sprang from the platform.

One other person saw Henri. With deadly accuracy, Calabash sent his banjo flying into the side of Henri's head. Then in a swift, waddling gait, he ran and threw himself at the back of Henri's knees. Henri collapsed in a heap. The guards were running toward the auctioneer whose fit of sneezing was so violent that he appeared to be having a seizure. I jumped on the midget's back seconds after he tackled Henri and pummeled him.

"Get up! Run!" I shouted at Henri.

Henri ran, knocking down people as he went, blood streaming down his face from the cut made by the banjo. Now the guards saw him, but were afraid to fire their muskets into the crowded hall. They rushed after him, no match for his long legs and disregard for spectators. Henri did not stop to open the inspection room door; he went through it as though it were made of paper. He drove his fist into the belly of Angèle's buyer, grabbed Angèle by the arm, and dragging her with him, leaped through the window to the ground six feet below. Three guards jammed the window in time to see Henri and Angèle gallop away on one of the horses that had been tied up in front of the hotel. One guard fired, but he had no chance of hitting them.

The midget and I sat on the floor of the rotunda staring hatefully at each other.

"You, girl," he said, "it was you! I know who you are and I'll tell!"

He scrambled to his feet, ran to the auctioneer, and began pulling on the tail of his coat. The auctioneer, still red-eyed, was trying to bring order out of chaos and paid no attention. Rapping his mallet on the stand, he shouted, "Calmez-vous! Do not excite yourselves! We will get them back, never fear, but meanwhile, we have many bargains for you!"

But although no one was badly hurt, the crowd had panicked. There was always fear of a black uprising, and something out of control like this was terrifying. The crowd dispersed, and the auctioneer had to lead the unsold slaves and the furious midget back to the pen.

And I was thinking, I did it! I did it! I have the Power and I made them escape! I am the future queen, and I can do anything! I went home, swollen with pride.

The next day there was an ad in the daily *Bee*:

FIFTY DOLLARS REWARD

WILL BE PAID FOR APPREHENSION AND DELIVERY to the subscriber of the Negro man, *Henri*, and the female, *Angèle*, who absented themselves on the morning of July 28. Said Negro is 25 years old and extremely tall. The female is slight, about 19 years of age, and of genteel appearance.

Captains of steamboats and vessels and any other persons are hereby cautioned against harbouring said slaves under the severest penalty of the law.

WM. N. FOUCHER
103 CONTI ST.

They sent dogs to track the runaways, but Henri was an outdoor man and he knew the land. He must have carried Angèle deep into the swamp. I heard that the dogs and men sent to capture them soon abandoned their search for fear of snakes and alligators.

When I told Dédé what had happened, she smiled, but when I bragged that I was the one who had done it all, she said, "What makes you so sure they won't still get caught? Or eaten by alligators? And anyhow, maybe it wasn't the gris-gris that worked; maybe Philomène said a prayer to the Virgin and the Virgin helped them escape. I don't think Damballah would do anything good for anyone. In fact, he probably helped the midget!"

"Dédé! Please don't say bad things about Damballah. He knows when you do."

"I don't care. I told you. He's a stupid snake and if he has any Power, it's evil because he's evil."

"He's heard you, Dédé. I know it. I'm going to him. I'll croon to him like Maman does, and I'll tell him you don't really mean it."

Damballah lay curled in a corner of his cage, his mean little eyes bright and knowing. Maman, being busy, had had little time for him and he was sulking. I brought him wine and honey, but he knew I did not really like him, and he stuck out his forked tongue and shook the tip of his tail. The thought came into my mind that he was reading the future and saw in it something terrible, which pleased him.

That night Dédé slept with Mère so that I could rest more comfortably and get rid of my headache. I stumbled wearily to our room alone, and opened the shutters. A leaf rustled in the windless dark, causing the back of my neck to prickle. What unwanted spirits had been released when I uncorked the gris-gris at the auction?

"Send them back!" I prayed into the oppressive night, and realized I was addressing God. He would not hear me—there it was again!—a feeling, a presence coming closer. I lay perfectly still, wishing Dédé were there. An acrid smell filled my nostrils. Moonlight broke the cloud cover, lit the room, and cast a misshapen shadow on the floor. On the windowsill, too solid for spirit, perched the midget Calabash, like a giant bird of prey, his eyes searching my room.

I tried to cry out, but something had happened to my voice. Calabash leaped to the foot of the bed and scrambled onto my chest.

"Ha, little sorceress, you succeeded, you think? Let me tell you how the story will end. If they have not already been eaten, I will catch them! How, you think? When they are deep in the swamp and even the dogs have failed? And I—just a small mistake of nature—I will *smell* them out. Just as I have you. Look!" He extended his arms, grotesquely as long and powerful as Henri's. "I will swing through the trees like a monkey, high above the snakes and alligators, and I will drop on them suddenly and silently." He jumped up and dropped back to the foot of my bed. "I will tie them up before they know what has happened. Snap! What delicious morsels they will be for the alligators." He paused to enjoy the picture he had conjured.

"And, little Voodoo queen, when you hear what has happened to your friends, you will know that *you did it to them*, and that I am on my way back for *you*."

With a cry of rage and a crablike movement, he reached the sill and flew through the window. It happened so quickly, I would have thought it a nightmare if it had not been for his lingering odor.

What had I done? What had made me think I could play at Voodoo? He would find them. He possessed the sharpened senses, the special power of misshapen people. What measure of Power did I have compared with the evil of Calabash? When speech came back to me, I could only moan. If I had not brought gris-gris to the auction, wouldn't Henri have gotten just as angry and wouldn't that anger have given him the same power my gris-gris had? If I had not meddled, the midget would not want to follow just two more escaped slaves. Never again! Never, never again would I meddle in Voodoo.

Over and over, through my headache, I thought the same muddled useless things, until finally, I fell asleep to dream I was back in the great auction hall of the St. Louis Hotel, where the sun shone through the tall windows on people called merchandise.

·❧[X V]❧··

Between Two Worlds

The sun had come out from behind a cloud and was shining in my eyes.

"Did you faint, Stephanie?" Annie was slapping my face. "Are you all right now?" she asked anxiously.

"I'm all right. What did I do?" I asked fearfully.

"You just closed your eyes. You were talking about Dédé one minute, then you just closed your eyes and I couldn't wake you. I was scared. And I didn't know what to do. I propped you against this tree, and finally I slapped you and you woke up."

"Annie, don't tell at school!"

"I won't tell," she promised earnestly.

I wondered why she cared about me, but it was enough that she did. We went back to Bois more subdued than we'd set out. I knew Annie was uneasy about keeping silent. I had put too much responsibility on her asking her not to tell.

"I don't mind for me," she said, "but maybe you need a doctor. Maybe you should talk to Mother Marie-Thérèse again."

The Chalk Cross

"All right. I'll talk to her." It took me a whole day to make up my mind to really go to the office, and then, when I walked in, I didn't know how to start.

"Reverend Mother, do you believe in spirits?" I blurted out.

She took hold of herself right away and answered, "Yes, I do, Stephanie! Spirit is as good a name as any for that part of us that is not flesh, nor even intelligence or emotion—the part that is a unique response to life. And it survives. I believe that."

"But, Reverend Mother, could I really experience another life?"

Mother Marie-Thérèse paused and then said slowly, "What is real, Stephanie? Isn't all experience real? Is the man I casually passed on the street yesterday more real to me than, say, Teresa of Avila who died hundreds of years ago but whose autobiography changed my life, changed me?" She fingered her rosary. "You might say I have lived two lives, each real and quite distinct. Or to put it another way, two spirits have inhabited my body. Isn't that what you're telling me is happening to you?"

It was, in a way, but there was more to it than that. The drawings—especially the drawings—had I done them? And if I was experiencing Donie's life, how was it being accomplished and why? God's hand at work and a maturing process, Mother Marie-Thérèse had suggested once before.

"But of course," Maman might have said. "It is the Power, chérie! And it is all the same what Père Antoine is saying and what I am telling you. Only the way of expressing it is different."

"The Power? Power of suggestion!" Sister Julie would say. "You have done nothing but work, read, write, and draw, all based on those early New Orleans years. The people, their customs—the very streets still here to walk through while your imagination runs wild ahead of you. You are so impressionable, Stephanie. You are simply identifying."

And Annie? How would she put it?

Mother Marie-Thérèse was looking at me sympathetically. "Stephanie, have faith—faith in yourself. You know, your friend Annie showed your portfolio to Mr. Dupuy this morning, and he showed it to me. 'You see, Reverend Mother,' " Mother Marie-Thérèse imitated Mr. Dupuy's abrupt speech, " 'it is not as desperate as I thought. This line here, the feeling in that face—it is *possible* we will *someday* have an artist.' "

She smiled as she watched my reaction to those precious words. "Now go along, child. I am meeting with the archdiocesan funding committee. Some of *them* could do with a second spirit!"

I found Annie in her room, cracking and eating pecans and struggling with her essay.

"I wish I could get involved just half as much as you do," she said as I came in. "My muse is not interested in 'Flora and Fauna of Louisiana' and there's just so much you can say about . . ."

"Annie, your plant drawings are beautiful. And, Annie, thank you for showing the drawings to Mr. Dupuy and saying they are mine. If *only* they are! But even so, you saved me from being sent back to my aunt's. Oh, the *thought* of that!

The Chalk Cross

"Stephanie, the drawings *are* yours. Remember?" She lifted one of her own. "But what do *I* do with these *beautiful* plant drawings, done by me without ghostly aid of any kind, portraying flora I can't identify? What is this, for instance? It's not in the reference book, and you know Sister Julie—I'll have to know the Latin name and all about it. . . ."

"It's rosemary!" I said. "How can you miss the smell? Listen, *I* know all about it—it's for remembrance and it used to be used medicinally for headaches and arthritis, but Maman used it to stay young, and now, it's delicious with chicken. I can tell you all sorts of stories about it."

"Perfect!" cried Annie, scribbling away. "What else?"

So I told Annie the legend of how, when Mary and Joseph were fleeing from Herod into Egypt, Mary's blue cloak brushed a rosemary bush and turned the white blossoms blue forever. As I told it, I remembered that the story had been told to me by Mère yesterday. *Yesterday?* It couldn't have been yesterday. I wasn't with Mère yesterday. I was *here*. STEPHANIE! I was slipping back, remembering another story Mère had told. NO, I would not go back! I resisted with all my strength, calling on the Power I hoped I had. If I kept myself from remembering the story, I wouldn't go back. But there was a reason I *had* to remember. It was terribly important, something to do with helping Dédé. Dédé was in trouble! . . .

"Donie!" Mère was saying. "Listen! I want to tell you a story."

"Now? Why now? I . . ."

"It has a bearing. Listen. Long ago, there lived in Africa a woman called Mignonette because she was so small, being only four feet high. Now she could conjure up any visions you might want to see, or not want to see if she chose to frighten you, for her knowings were as old as Africa itself.

"One day, a white man with beautiful red beads lured her onto a slave ship, and she spent many years in captivity—here in this city. Finally, when she was very old, she earned her freedom by helping her master free his son from the Calaboose, where he awaited hanging, having been sentenced to die for murder. She conjured up a vision of the boy for the jailers to hold in prison and hang while the real son went home with his father. Yes, she could do things that today are no longer understood, but are lost forever.

"When Mignonette became old and could no longer get about, I brought her gumbo on Sundays and helped her bathe and dress. One day she said to me, 'You so good to me, ma chère, I would like to repay you. I will teach you my finest spell, how when someone is asleep and their soul has left their body to wander through the dream world, you can capture that soul and do with it what you will!'

"And so she told me the ingredients of the gris-gris and taught me the words of the chant, and shortly after that, she died."

Mère paused thoughtfully.

"Yes, Mère?" I asked impatiently. "What has that to do with me?"

"I used that spell only once," she continued. "There

was an evil woman, always doing mischief to others, and one time she put a viper in the leg of a friend of mine, a good woman. That night when the evil woman's wicked spirit-soul was out dreaming, I came into her room and captured it and drove it deep into a snail shell, plugged the shell with clay and jammed it tight in the knothole of an old oak tree. That woman never did mischief again. She just walked through the rest of her life like a zombi, and even when she died, I did not free her spirit for fear it would soon find another body."

Mère stopped again.

"Mère, what does it mean? What has that story to do with me?" I asked while at the back of my mind, I thought, "I am Stephanie. No, I must be Donie because I'm talking to Mère. NO, I AM STEPHANIE." And that thought was so strong, Mère left before telling me the meaning of the story.

"Stephanie! Are you there?" Annie asked. "You look a million miles away."

"I'm here," I answered. I was thinking I'd *made myself* return. Had the initiation worked for me after all? I had controlled the coming back part! I would need to do it again because I *had* to go back. I had to find out why Mère had told me that story.

When I was alone in my room, I felt an urgency about the familiar tugging. I remembered the wistful look of Donie's portrait. What was it she wanted? And what did Mère want? Why did I think it had to do with Dédé?

I opened one of my reference books at random and read words written by a visitor to New Orleans during the great epidemic of 1832:

. . . I found the graveyard a large pile of corpses without coffins, in horizontal layers, one above the other like cordwood. . . . Large trenches were dug, into which these uncoffined corpses were thrown indiscriminately. The same day a private hospital was found deserted; the physicians, nurses, and attendants were all dead or had run away. . . .

That was it! *I remembered that day!*

From the street, over the convent wall, and across the herb garden and time, I heard the rumble of cart wheels and a driver's voice shout, "Bring out your dead!" I put my fingers in my ears to shut out the terrible words, but that only increased my sense of smell, and I smelled something frightening and familiar—I smelled the plague.

⦗XVI⦘

The Plague

The oppressive weather made my headache worse. A damp blanket of heat covered the city, and low, thick clouds kept it so dark, we had to light candles at noon. Not a breath of air stirred the gauze curtains, and fear of the pestilence was everywhere. "One out of six will die this year," they whispered.

The smells of the city vied with each other. The heavy perfume of the sweet olive alternated with the stench of the waste-filled gutters. The honeysuckle entwined with the odor of roasting coffee. The river smelled of itself; and the docks, of grain, cotton, spices, and salted fur skins. In the heart of the city, the café smell of stale wine, Havana cigars, and wet straw met the sticky odor of cane being boiled into molasses. A blind man could tell the city's story by his nose. But when the yellow fever struck, there was only one smell. It was everywhere; it clung in the nostrils, and if you let it, it crept over the body, claiming it for the grave. It was the smell of death.

No one left home unless it was absolutely necessary.

The Plague

Shops closed and the only movements in the streets were the waves of heat rising from the cobblestones and the carts that rolled endlessly along carrying the dead, too numerous for individual burial, to a place outside the city where the corpses were dumped into ditches and covered with mud; the "wet grave" it was called, and there were fearful whispers of hasty burials that turned out to be premature.

At the street corners, barrels of tar and pitch burned to purify the air, and cannons were fired for the same purpose. But a foul-smelling miasma hung over the city. There was no place in the narrow streets to hide from the stench; it seeped through the closed shutters into the house. I pressed a sweet-olive blossom to my nose, but its cloying perfume only made me more nauseated.

I did not sleep well at night; I lay listening for Calabash. When I did fall asleep, I had nightmares, and I had dreamed the same one twice. Mère says that if you dream something three nights in a row, it will come true. In my dream, I am standing at a gate, knocking. I want urgently to go through the gate, but I don't know why or what is on the other side. I knock harder. The gate turns to stone. I *must* get in! I push with all my weight and the stone door grinds open, but my excitement jolts me out of sleep before I've learned the secret, and I feel as tired as when I first went to bed.

Maman was also not getting enough rest. She was helping Père Antoine nurse and comfort the dying and came home for short periods only. "Donie, how is your headache? Dédé, help Mère fix a light supper. No meat but use salt and spice plentifully and drink the juice of at least one lemon mixed with cream of tartar. And wear your flannel shirts so that you will perspire freely."

Maman made us wear flannel shirts night and day, days that seemed as much a part of the dream world as the night.

It was seven nights after Calabash had been in my room, and I still had not heard anything about Angèle and Henri. I was deep in sleep, the way you are when you have only been asleep a short time. Something waked me and I knew immediately it was a sound from outside. Calabash had finished with Angèle and Henri and was coming for me.

"Donie! Donie, it's me, Angèle!"

I jumped out of bed and helped her through the window. I could see Henri crouched under the fig tree in our garden.

"Calabash—the midget—he is after you! Why did you come back?"

"Donie, he came at us! From above, high in the trees! He was following us and Henri knew it, only he thought it was some kind of wild cat. Who would have thought a man? You know what a clever woodsman Henri is! Well, he heard this *thing*, but he did not look around or give any sign he was warned. He strung the bow and arrow he had made and just as Calabash sprang from the tree, Henri spun around. His arrow caught Calabash straight through the heart and he was dead in seconds. Henri buried him with prayers and tears. Imagine! I can tell you *I* didn't cry!"

"But why did you come back? You'll be caught—and Henri, too!"

"I can't leave without Philomène, Donie! I want you to tell her we are hiding close by and will take her with us. There is a man, a farmer, one of many men and women who call themselves the underground railroad, and it goes all the way north to freedom. If you can get Philomène out of the marquis's house, we will bring her too."

"Angèle, I can't do that! She is like a zombi. You know yourself! I . . ."

"Donie, listen! You have the *Power*. Didn't you make our escape? Of course you can do it! You need only the right gris-gris."

The right gris-gris! How could I tell Angèle that I was not sure I had the Power? How could I say that even if I had it, it seemed to work against me and I didn't want to use it anymore? I couldn't refuse so I said, "Angèle, I'll try."

She grabbed my hand. "You'll do it!" she said confidently. "You have the Power! We'll come back tomorrow night." And she climbed back out the window to Henri.

The next morning, I wondered if Angèle had been a vision. I lay lethargic; it was only seven o'clock, but already the terrible heat was squeezing the strength out of me and my flannel shirt was sopping wet with sweat. My headache was only biding its time, waiting to rush into my head and fill it. I forced myself up, washed, dressed, and went out into the stinking street. There was no use consulting Damballah. We did not trust each other. I had no plans, no idea what I would do when I got to the marquis's house. You cannot make gris-gris out of thin air, and I felt not a shred of Power.

The Chalk Cross

I was holding my nose, afraid to breathe, when I turned a corner and saw the marquis's door. There, above his crest in bronze, hung a wreath tied with black ribbon. Voodoo—God—somebody or something had worked! The marquis was dead! I ran down the alley to the back. In the courtyard, I saw Cook, her eyes red from weeping.

"Ah, Donie," she began sobbing. "So young and beautiful! Such a waste! But so unhappy. All for the best, maybe, for *he*," she spat, "he lives—he eats and drinks and drinks and drinks and eats—and may God keep her bright soul in peace from *him*."

I was already so full of regrets, there was no room for anything else, not even grief for Philomène, one more dead in the city of the dead.

"The two of them gone!" said Cook. "One so white and fair, the other so dark and beautiful! Both my babies lost!"

I could not let her think Angèle was dead too. I told Cook she was safe and that I'd seen her, but I did not mention the underground railroad. The fewer people who knew about that, the safer Angèle and Henri were.

"Ah, thank God for that, thank God!" said Cook fervently. "And you, child, take care, my pet. Go home quickly. Yellow Jack walks the streets." She crossed herself and backed away from me.

I was on my way home when I saw a girl who looked so much like me, I thought I was seeing myself. I started to speak to her, but when I got close, I stumbled. I reached out to keep from falling and caught the brass rail of my bed at Bois.

Me! She was seeing me, Stephanie. I had walked those

streets. I hadn't even had a warning this time; I had less control than ever and was snapping back and forth on a thought. I must not go back again, not for anything. Yellow Jack is there! I cannot go home!

"Home is here at Bois," I said aloud. Even as I said the words, I knew that home was the cottage on St. Ann Street and that Maman was waiting for me.

Maman had slept for less than an hour, and hollow circles ringed her eyes. She looked at me and said, "Rest awhile."

She made an incense of rosemary and juniper, and rubbed my forehead with vinaigre des quatre valeurs, mumbling a chant as she massaged. She said she did not believe I had the fever. "Yellow Jack gallops through the body. Your headache is merely strolling."

I was not so sure and I was afraid for Maman too.

"No. I will not be ill," she said.

"How can you be certain, 'ti Maman?" I asked.

"I am sure," she answered, with the certainty she had in telling the future.

She looked at me closely. "You feel sick from the fumes of the mal-aria, but I do not think you will get the fever. When you've rested, go to the apothecary and get cinchona and tartar emetic."

"Oui, Maman," I answered. These were medicines to fight yellow fever, so if she thought I did not have the fever, for whom did she need the medicine?

"Now eat," Mère said to Dédé. "You've got to have your strength or you'll wilt like a plucked flower."

Dédé's legs were skinny under the dress Mère had stitched for her.

"I'm not hungry," Dédé said.

Dédé! Of course! It was Dédé they feared for! Dédé, frail, always the sickly one. Oh, please, not Dédé! I cannot stand it if she gets the fever. Let it be *me*!

Mère passed the comb through Dédé's hair and tried to hide the huge ball of it that came out. A wave of fear nauseated me and I left the room.

Still nauseated, I looked at Annie.

"Annie, don't stay! You'll get the fever! You'll . . ."

"Stephanie, what are you talking about?"

Annie, wasn't *there*—I was *here*, in her room at Bois.

"Annie, who am I?" I asked desperately. "Am I Stephanie or Sidonie?"

Annie put her head to the side and her finger to her chin. "Let me see, now, when I first met you, you were Stephanie, stuffy and snobby. Now you smile occasionally, and as I pointed out to you, you look exactly like Marie Laveau's daughter. So my guess is you've done a Dr. Jekyll and Mr. Hyde. Or is it Mr. Jekyll and Dr. Hyde? I can never remember."

"It's not funny," I said, hearing the panic in my voice. "I'm serious."

"You're too serious."

"But it isn't normal. I'm Stephanie, but—but, I'm Donie too! Something is happening!"

Annie gave a big sigh. "All right. Look, why don't you just accept the fact of *you*, as you are now, and go on from there?"

Because, I thought dizzily, I am not yet a fact. I must know who I am.

"Tell me some more about rosemary," said Annie. "I

need five hundred words and this is only three hundred and seventy-five."

"All right, but listen, one more thing—" If I keep talking, I thought, I will not go back. I must not go back to that terrible time. "I still have a drawing to do, and I don't know if I can do it. It really may have been Donie . . ."

"Well, if it was Donie and you are Donie now, then you ought to draw just as well as she did before," said Annie impatiently. "Tell yourself or tell her to draw something—something she knows and cares about, to quote a certain teacher, and tell her not to leave out the bones, to quote another."

Something she cares about. The initiation—how had that *really* been? I hurried to my room and began to draw the initiation as I remembered it. I put myself into it, dancing in the circle on the chalk cross with Maman and Damballah and even Zouzou watching me. I felt again the wild rhythm of the Calinda and heard the urgency of the drums. I was living it; I was drawing it; it was my life and my drawing, and I saw then that I must have fallen outside the circle, because there was the stone I'd hit my head on, well beyond the line. And I knew with terrifying certainty that only Maman had the Power. I have no control, I thought; I am at the mercy of the Power, and something is stealing over me with a strength far beyond my resistance. The Power? Fear? Or the yellow fever?

The daily newspaper, *The Bee,* said fear was a predisposing agent for yellow fever. That meant you were more likely to get the disease if you were afraid than if you were not. But how could you not fear Yellow Jack, or the Black Vomit as it was sometimes called?

The very names made shivers down the spine. Yellow Jack had once appeared to me in a dream and I knew his true form was a yellow skeleton dressed in rags. He rode through the streets on a nag, pointing a boney finger at one, then another, calling, "You!" and "You!" and cackling as he watched the victim clutch his aching head. Then came the terrible stomach cramp and the chill, followed by fever. After that, a respite from all symptoms, during which the patient hoped he was recovering. But Yellow Jack was only gathering strength for the kill. Now, he marched through the body, turning it as yellow as his own. Once the victim vomited black—described accurately as a substance resembling coffee grounds—there was no hope left and death came quickly. Not to be afraid of such a terror? It was impossible.

I walked down the cobbled street to the apothecary, past closed shops and shuttered windows. Lighted street-lamps were strung between the iron balconies and cast a thin shadow of me as I walked. The gutters were being cleaned by river water let in through holes in the levee. The water rushed along carrying the waste to the swamps beyond the city, and it was from there, the doctors said, that foul miasmas were born and rose to blanket the city with mal-aria and pestilence.

Every day since the first cases had been reported, more and more horrible stories were told. There was a bride, married in the morning, buried in the afternoon still dressed in her wedding veil; a young man, interred alive, found too late, his fingers stiff and curved from clawing at the lid of his coffin. Each tale fed the fear already present.

When I reached Philippe's old apothecary shop, it was closed and there was a notice on the door that said the new proprietor had the fever. As I turned away, the cathedral bell began tolling the matins, sending the pigeons fluttering around the tower. It seemed like an omen and I decided to go in. I went through the side portal, careful to dip my fingers in the holy water held in a vase for that purpose. I made the sign of the cross as Père Antoine had taught us to do to ward off evil. I did not believe it was quite as potent as salt in a cross, but it helped.

I made my way carefully from pillar to pillar toward the main altar, genuflecting before the statues of the saints in every niche. The Virgin Mary, standing on a side altar, was the most beautiful. She had been made in Paris by a famous artist. Her skin was luminous, her cheeks tinted pink, and her eyes blue indigo. She had real yellow curls topped with a jeweled gold crown. Her dress was the same blue as her eyes and trimmed with more gold. Beneath one dainty foot, she trampled a snake, Satan, and I was startled by its resemblance to Damballah.

In the shadows, someone else knelt and prayed before the image of the Virgin. It was Maman! Her hands were clasped and stretched forward, and from her mouth, closed on protruding red peppers, came a humming chant like the sound of bees swarming. She was asking the Virgin to do something for her, something needing the kind of power she did not have. Quickly, I turned and made my way back down the aisle. Once outside, I raced home.

I found Dédé doubled up with stomach cramps. Denaud was crouched in a corner of her room, his bright spirit subdued for once, and Mère was bending over Dédé, stroking her forehead.

Maman came in behind me.

"*Make her well, Maman!*" I screamed.

"Donie! One of the things I try hardest to teach you is not to lose control. Do not let the Power escape in every direction like a firecracker going off. Channel it. Now, let us quietly make the gris-gris together."

"I can't, Maman! I don't have the Power! You have the Power. I don't. If ever I had it, Damballah took it back after I helped Angèle escape. Maybe he doesn't like her; I don't know. I only know I feel nothing."

"You helped Angèle escape?"

"Yes. I was no help to Philomène, but I *did* help Angèle and Henri escape."

"Donie, I don't believe it! First, you went against the Power I brought in, and then you caused someone to lose what he had paid for? His property?"

"Maman, I do not believe people are things that can be bought and sold. How would you like to be owned and have some fat man take Denaud away and sell him where we'd never see him again or even know if he were alive or . . ."

"Donie, you are being absurd. We are *free*, not slaves. If anyone did that to us, he would be a kidnapper, and kidnappers are subject to severe punishment as you know. It would be against the law, entirely different."

"Oh, Maman, don't you see? The law is *wrong*!"

"The law is wrong? Donie, that is dangerous talk. Next, you will be saying Père Antoine is wrong too. It is a stage you are going through, chérie; I see you are still too young to understand fully but I can tell you this. You do have the Power. I myself passed it on to you. So now we will use it together. Fetch Damballah."

I walked slowly into the garden. I did not believe Damballah would help Dédé. I did not think he would do Maman's will if he knew she had prayed to the Virgin.

I started back into the house carrying Damballah's cage, but quickly hid him behind my back when I heard the voice of Père Antoine.

"Please come, Madame Laveau," he was begging. "Only for a short time, and then you can return to Dédé. We have found the hospital on Canal Street completely deserted by the attendants and I need your help."

"Bien sûr, Mon Père," Maman murmured. "Un moment." She came out of the room to me and whispered, "You must do it, Donie. Here." She gave me the two red peppers I had seen in her mouth when she prayed in the cathedral. "Put these under Dédé's pillow." She caught my shoulders. "You can do it, Donie, believe me. I will be back as soon as possible."

And with that she left me holding Damballah's cage in one hand and the peppers in the other. I looked down at the peppers in my hand. If they had any meaning for Maman, she would have to use them. They had none for me. I could not feel a speck of Power in me. I left the peppers on a table in the hall.

I looked at Damballah and he returned my look coldly. Then his eyes shifted to the peppers and he hissed and shook. He would not help Dédé or me. He had always hated Dédé, and now he had turned against me. He lay limp in his cage.

"I hate you," I said, with all the loathing I had always felt. I brought him back into the garden, gave his cage a good shake, and came inside in time to hear Dédé say, "Mère, I am so tired. I want to sleep."

"Then, sleep, chérie, my sweet. It is the best medicine of all."

After Dédé had fallen asleep, Mère turned to me and said, "It is the pause before the end begins," and I knew she meant Yellow Jack would return to claim Dédé.

"NO!" I cried. "Fight, Dédé! Don't give in!" But she was too deep in sleep to hear me.

"Donie, chère, I am thinking," said Mère.

"Thinking? What are you thinking?" I yelled rudely.

"I am thinking that although I have not used the Power for years, I still know Mignonette's spell. You remember the story I told you?"

"Yes, yes! But what good will that do now?"

"Well, chère, I am thinking that before Dédé goes into the last of this terrible sickness, sure to end in death, I could capture her spirit while she sleeps and is dreaming away from her body, and you could send it to God where she so much wants to go. Then, only the shell of her body would go through the terrible act of dying. What do you think?"

"No! No, I won't do that! I don't want Dédé to die! I won't let her die!"

"Chère, you have lost her already. Can't you see Yellow Jack has her?"

I looked. Then I closed my eyes tight and asked in a whisper, "How do I send Dédé to God?"

"Didn't Père Antoine teach you the proper spell—or prayer as he calls it?" asked Mère, amazed at my question.

"There is a prayer asking God to take the soul of the dying—but God does not always do what you ask of Him."

"Even with the proper words?"

"Père Antoine says He does what is best."

"Then He will surely take Dédé."

And so Mère mixed the gris-gris, which had in it asafetida and something with an acrid smell that she kept hidden in her armoire. Then Mère chanted an incantation, a long and difficult one with high, whining notes and words from the forgotten language. I almost ruined it all by whispering once more, "Please try, Dédé! Fight!"

But Yellow Jack would not let her go, and while Dédé slept and her spirit roamed the dream world, Mère sprinkled the gris-gris on her pillow, and when Dédé's spirit tried to come back into her body, Mère held it gently and I choked out the prayer which ended, "Go, Spirit of Dédé, go to God!" Dédé called my name as her spirit left, and it was as Mère wanted it to happen: the body went through the last phases of yellow fever, but Dédé was already gone.

Something of Mère left too; it was as though she had only been waiting for Dédé. She looked like an empty shell.

The Chalk Cross

I felt nothing. I thought if only I can hold myself like this, I will never have to feel again. I will not let go. Even when Angèle appeared that night and I had to tell her that she and Henri would travel the railroad alone, it did not upset me. Each of us was alone, locked in separate rooms of grief.

We buried Dédé in our family tomb, a luxury not granted to many in that time of death and mass burial. Just before we closed the coffin—a hastily made pine one—I saw Maman place the red peppers next to Dédé. Then Maman closed her eyes and moved her lips silently, but whether she was saying prayers or incantations, I did not care. Père Antoine said the burial prayers, and although he had seen so many die, he had tears for Dédé. As the coffin was placed in the tomb-house, he said,

> *Men's days are like the grass;*
> *he blossoms like the flowers*
> *of the field; a wind passes*
> *over them, and they cease to be*
> *and their place knows them no more.*

We left the cemetery. I did not cry and I did not pray. I did what I had to do like a zombi until I came home to our room, neat and clean, with every trace of Dédé erased forever. My spirit hovered outside me somewhere, afraid to come back into my body, for when it did, the body would go wild with grief.

I would never care about anything or anyone again. I understood everything because there was nothing to understand. Then, into the nothingness someone reached out to me and I thought I heard my name called. I could

no longer hold out. Words that were not mine answered
for me . . .

> *God, let my cry for help reach you!*
> *Do not hide your face from me*
> *For I am in distress!*

sang the nuns in the chapel.

> *Lord make haste and give me answer*
> *for my spirit fails within me.*
> *Do not hide your face*
> *lest I become like those in the grave.*

I was sitting in the herb garden with a pencil in my
hand. I could not draw. The plague was too terrible, too
personal and involving, and I could not draw anything
connected with it. The grave was terrifying; I could
see it, smell it even, stronger than the scent of the
herbs.

But why should I be afraid of the grave? I am
Stephanie, strong, well, living now—far away from fear
of yellow fever. I could draw what I pleased. I didn't have
to draw the plague. I started drawing one thing, then
another, erasing, that unforgivable sin, over and over.

From somewhere had come a drawing of the auction.
There was the mean little encanteur, pounding his gavel,
his lips forming the word, "Sold!" Among the slaves on
the block stood Angèle looking brave, Henri looking
fearful, and Calabash watching him. Donie was lost in
the crowd. She had not yet uncorked the bottle. The
drawing was Donie's, and must have been done long ago
for I was Stephanie now. I was an artist. I couldn't draw a

line. I'd *done* this drawing. No, that was Donie and Stephanie *couldn't draw*!

The air had grown still in the garden, waiting for the afternoon thundershower. Even the birds were quiet. I heard a distant roll of thunder that sounded like drums. A heavy cloud shut out the sun, making the day dark and weighing down on me. Another roll of thunder. I must go inside. No, it wasn't thunder; it was drums, and I was already inside my room on St. Ann Street.

·◦[XVII]◦·

The Other Side
of the Door

A sudden breeze, the first in days, blew the candle out. I looked out of the window and saw a curtain of dark clouds rising from the south. A storm was coming and on the first breeze rode the sound of drums. At first they were only the usual ones sending messages from one house to another. Then as the storm grew, the drums became louder, their great, long notes thumping against the walls of the house.

Damballah lay curled, his head high, listening. He began to move in a way I'd never seen before. He swayed to the rhythm of the drums, and as he went from side to side, he seemed to be blowing himself up, getting larger, growing out of his cage, until the noise almost burst my ears and he was twenty feet long, high and menacing over my head.

But as he grew, so did my hate for him, and my hate outgrew my fear until there was only hate. I dived into his exposed underside and he collapsed like a punctured balloon back into his cage, only a snake. I did not have the Power, but neither did he.

The Chalk Cross

I grabbed the cage and ran with it out of the house. The wind beat me from every direction and rain slapped needle blows against my face. The drums had become the sound of the storm crushing against my head. At the end of the street, the road turned to slosh and with each step, my feet sank deep in the mud. The trees, buffeted by wind, swooped down at me. I could barely see where I was going and the little I saw looked unfamiliar.

I came at last to what I thought must be the secret Voodoo place, although the bayou was swollen beyond recognition. The water was black and the current swift, carrying with it bobbing things of all kinds. I looked around for something heavy, found a stone, and pried it loose from the ground. I opened the door of Damballah's cage just enough to slip the stone in. Damballah threw himself from side to side, hissing at me and flicking his tongue at my hand. I planted my feet firmly on the bank, swung the cage behind me, and heaved Damballah far out to the middle of the racing bayou.

"*Now*, Damballah," I screamed in the wind, "do your magic!"

The wind howled louder than ever making me dizzy with what sounded like the roar of elephants stampeding toward me. The bayou, mottled with debris, heaved and writhed like a giant snake. It was curling toward me. I stood paralyzed as the huge mouth of Damballah opened and swallowed me. I was tossed upside down in the current and sucked under to the bottom.

I have heard that just before you drown, your whole life passes before you, and as my lungs began to fill, I thought of everyday things that made up my life, of

Maman's candlelit face as she told the future, of Père Antoine patiently answering my questions, of Mère's gingerbread, dripping with butter and syrup, of Denaud bouncing on my bed, shouting, "I'm ready, Donie! Let's go to the levee!", of Dédé laughing quietly at him, and of the feel of chalk between my fingers and the look of white paper . . . clean and white . . . waiting for a line . . . white paper . . .

White paper . . . bright in the dark herb garden. I was safe! The threatening sky didn't matter, because I was here at Bois, and I was only trying to *draw* that other terrible time. I was Stephanie, safe in the present.

Then before I could finish my sigh of relief, I realized Donie was drowning! She wouldn't even try to save herself because she didn't think she had a future. But she did! I knew it because it was my future too. Suddenly, something else hit me with the force of a gigantic wave—I needed her as desperately as she needed me! What could I do here far away in time from what I knew best—from the reality of the past that belonged to me?

The will to live swept through me. It carried me back on its strong current to the bayou bottom, where with all my strength, I struggled out of my shroud of mud, pushed to the surface, and gulped air. I fought my way through the current to the bank and fell exhausted on the earth.

All around me was the silence that is the center of the storm. Only the bayou rushed noisily on. I must have lost consciousness, for when I opened my eyes the storm was swirling around me again and Maman was bending over me.

"Donie, what have you done? You have destroyed my Power!" Her voice faltered. "And your own future as queen."

"Maman, I have only killed a snake. Your Power is within you, and—and—I have no future without Dédé."

"Donie, my darling, that is no way to talk. Of course, you have a future. And it is not without Dédé. Did you not see me place the peppers with the Virgin's magic in her casket?"

"Maman, the peppers mean nothing."

"Ah, Donie, you have no faith. There is no Power without belief. But the spirit? You believe in that?" she asked almost timidly.

I nodded.

"Then remember how once you asked me about spirits inhabiting the same body? Dédé will always be with you."

It was the first thing Maman had ever said about the spirit world that I could believe.

"And my Power . . . ," Maman stopped. For once she seemed less than certain about something. "My Power— perhaps Damballah was not always good, but he helped me. He knew the future. Yes, that was his great strength. He knew the future."

"Then, he must have known I would never be queen!"

"Yes, that's true, and he tried to tell me. If I'd listened . . . Ah, but that is past. Now he is gone and it is possible that I will not see the future so clearly, but maybe it is enough to know the past. And it is true: I feel the Power still. It has always been part of me." Maman had become confident again. "What is it Père Antoine said to you about different beliefs?"

"That God has many faces you mean?"

"Yes, yes, that is it."

"Maman, I could not love the face of his that you see. We are so different."

"I understand that now, Donie, and what I want to say is that your future belongs to you. I could not take it away from you, and I am sorry now that I tried. Do you know I did it only from love?"

"Oh, yes, Maman! I have always known that."

"I could not take it away from you, but I can send you into it." She said this with her characteristic confidence and her look of concentration and impending power.

Silently, Maman drew in red chalk a cross on the exposed root of the oak. Then she lifted me onto it, and placing her hands on my head, she began the chant I'd heard her sing in the cathedral. She was calling someone far away, pleading, praying. I thought I caught the words "Grand Zombi," then, "Chère Vierge," but as I crouched against the tree, out of the wind, Maman's humming chant made me drowsy and I felt the Power. I knew the Power was not mine; it belonged to Maman, but it wrapped me round like a warm cloak, comforting and protecting me against the journey I had to make.

I dreamed I could fly, not with wings but with the same swimming movement I'd used to come to the surface of the bayou. I flew away from the storm and home, looking down on a changing landscape with people moving about. No one seemed to notice me even when I stopped to rest on rooftops. Sometimes I met others flying, but we did not speak. I heard voices but they did not belong to the faces I saw floating past. The voices blended into a kind of buzzing that I drifted in and out of. I heard my name called but that too had changed. I was no longer me, Donie. I was outside my body, wandering through a treeless, misty dreamworld.

A door appeared before me and I recognized it as the stone door of my dream. I pushed with all my strength, and it swung open easily. This time I went all the way through to the other side of a tomb-house where I sat drawing in the sun.

Epilogue

I drew a tomb-house. My hand led my thoughts, and I saw I'd drawn with two powerful strokes a red chalk cross on the stone steps and a girl leaning against the door of the tomb. As I darkened her hair with my pencil, I put the finishing touches on a self-portrait. I got up and walked back to Bois and through the gates into the herb garden. Sister Julie was hurrying toward me.

"There you are! Where have you been? You missed breakfast and assembly. . . . Stephanie, are you all right?"

"I'm fine. I'm finished."

"Finished?"

"My ten drawings."

Sister Julie took two new drawings from my hand. "Why it's St. Louis Cemetery! Who is this?" She pointed to the figure of a girl in front of a tomb-house, and without waiting for an answer, she looked at the other drawing and said, "Here she is again, flying over the city—how strange! Why is she doing that? Who is she?"

"That's me. I'm not really flying. I'm moving through time."

The Chalk Cross

Sister Julie looked at me in undisguised fear.

"It's like a journey," I tried to explain. "Only instead of arriving at a different place, you arrive in a different time. Sister Julie, don't look like that! I'm all right! And the strange part is all finished now—the going back, I mean." I heard Maman's kind of certainty in my own voice. It was true that I would never again go back, because I didn't have to. Donie's life was my past and she shared my future.

"Sister Julie, really, it's all right! You'll see."

My confidence touched her and she answered uncertainly, "Yes, but . . . Reverend Mother should . . ."

"I know. I know. I'll talk to her."

And, I'd tell Annie too, that I could accept me. I did not have the Power, but I didn't need it. I knew who I was and I could go on from there.